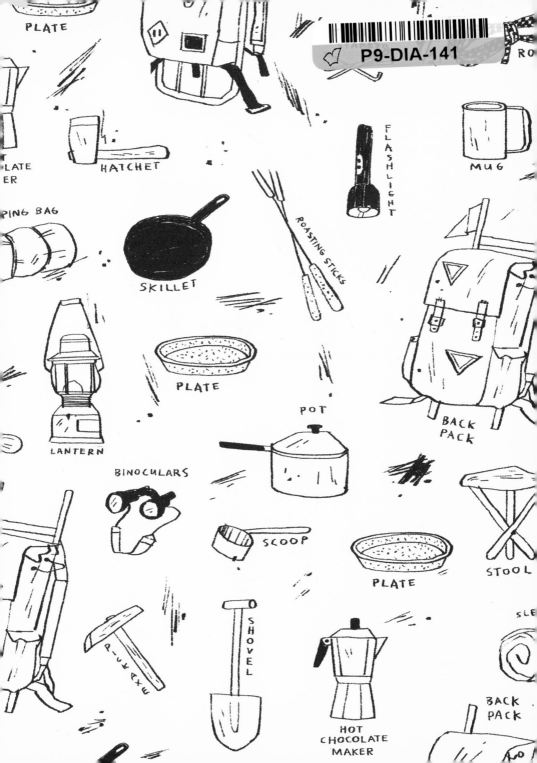

*Badger? Are you in there? Badger?*

# EGG
# MARKS
## *the*
# SPOT

*A Skunk and Badger Story*

## ALSO BY AMY TIMBERLAKE

*Skunk and Badger*

*One Came Home*
a Newbery Honor book
an Edgar Award winner

*That Girl Lucy Moon*

*The Dirty Cowboy*
illustrated by Adam Rex

# EGG
# MARKS
## *the*
# SPOT

*A Skunk and Badger Story*

*by* Amy Timberlake

*with pictures by* Jon Klassen

ALGONQUIN YOUNG READERS   2021

Published by
Algonquin Young Readers
an imprint of Algonquin Books of Chapel Hill
Post Office Box 2225
Chapel Hill, North Carolina 27515-2225

a division of
Workman Publishing
225 Varick Street
New York, New York 10014

Text © 2021 by Amy Timberlake.
Illustrations © 2021 by Jon Klassen.
Printed in China.
Design by Carla Weise.

LIBRARY OF CONGRESS CATALOGING-IN-PUBLICATION DATA
Names: Timberlake, Amy, author. | Klassen, Jon, illustrator.
Title: Egg marks the spot / by Amy Timberlake ; with pictures by Jon Klassen.
Description: First edition. | Chapel Hill, North Carolina : Algonquin
Young Readers, 2021. | Series: A Skunk and Badger story
Summary: "Roommates Skunk and Badger head out on a rock-finding expedition that
becomes much more dangerous than they ever expected"–Provided by publisher.
Identifiers: LCCN 2021007548 | ISBN 9781643750064 (hardcover) |
ISBN 9781643752280 (ebook)
Subjects: CYAC: Badgers–Fiction. | Skunks–Fiction. | Rocks–Fiction. | Dinosaurs–
Fiction. | Animals–Fiction. | Adventure and adventurers–Fiction. Classification:
LCC PZ7.T479 Eg 2021 | DDC [Fic]–dc23
LC record available at https://lccn.loc.gov/2021007548]

10 9 8 7 6 5 4 3 2 1
First Edition

*For Phil*

# EGG MARKS
## *the*
# SPOT

*A Skunk and Badger Story*

# CHAPTER ONE

RAP-RAP. RAP-RAP-RAP. THE KNOCKING SOUNDED ON the attic door, the door of Badger's new rock room.

It was his roommate, Skunk. Badger would ignore it. *He will go away*, he thought. *Important Rock Work—focus, focus, focus.* Badger gritted his teeth and leaned forward on his rock stool. He adjusted his special work light and lifted the unidentified object on his rock table.

He glanced at the list in his Important Rock Work notebook:

— igneous?
— granular groundmass — greenish
— red phenocrysts VERY SPARKLY

He looked at the object. He read the list again. He ran his paw over one of the object's phenocrysts, and thought, *It is time.*

Yes, it was time for the first question: Rock or mineral? Mineral or rock? Minerals were made of one basic material—one element or "an elemental compound," as the rock scientists said. There tended to be a sameness about a mineral. A rock, though, was a combination—a combination of minerals, or a combination of rocks and minerals. Two minerals stuck together? Rock. Five minerals scrambled up with a rock chucked in? Also, a rock.

The question, rock or mineral, was best asked loudly. It was followed by tossing the object into the air. When Badger caught the object, he would yell out the answer in a thunderous voice.

Badger's ears twisted in the door's direction. *No sounds.* So Badger opened his mouth, inhaled, and—

*Rap-rap-rap.*

The rapping was insistent—always, it insisted.

Badger exhaled and waited for what he knew would come next.

It came: "Badger?" *Rap-rap. Rap.*

Badger set his head upon the rock table. He had thought that moving his rock room from the living room to an out-of-the-way place, like the attic, would help. *Strategic!* he had thought

2

at the time. Back then, a tug on the chain of the attic's one bare bulb revealed a jumble of cardboard boxes, broken luggage, an assortment of odd furniture, an aquarium, a stack of oil paintings, and a claw-footed bathtub filled with hats.

Badger rotated his head to one side and spied the bathtub. The bathtub had refused to budge, so Badger had left the bathtub's third of the attic full of jumble and declared it useful storage with the added benefit of buffering the sound of his rock tumbler. Then he cleared out the remaining two-thirds for his rock room.

Out of the jumble had come a chair and a reading lamp. The pool table worked wonderfully well for rolling out geological survey maps, and the umbrella stand for storing them. Badger had utilized the attic cabinetry, lining drawers with soft velvet for hand lenses and magnifying glasses, his pocket utility knife, his scrapers and bradawls, his fine dust puffer. He'd hung hooks for hammers and chisels. Only when all this had been accomplished had Badger lugged his boxes of rocks and minerals, his table, his stool, and his work light up the two flights of stairs to the attic. "Weeks of work," Badger groaned.

*Rap-rap-rap! Rap!* "Badger? Are you in there? Badger?"

Badger ignored this and let his eyes take in what had once been a long, windowless wall. Badger had lined that wall with shelves. He'd installed light after tiny light. He'd written out name cards and found suitable stands—one for each specimen.

Badger lifted his head. He pushed back from the rock table. The wheels of his stool clattered over the uneven floorboards.

"Badger, is that you?"

Badger stood. The stool jostled.

*Rap-rap!*

Badger walked to the wall and flipped the light switch.

Behold, Badger's Wall of Rocks! Under each light a specimen shone—the exceptional, the one-of-a-kind, the rare and unrivaled. The copper shimmered. The mica sparked. The labradorite pulsed with color like some translucent deep-sea fish. "Yes," Badger whispered. Then his eyes alighted upon the empty stand at the beginning of his Wall of Rocks, and he felt a searing pain. He quickly looked away.

A muttering from the other side of the door: "It sounds like he is in there. He is not in his room. He is not downstairs. He is definitely not in the kitchen—where he always is."

Badger frowned. *I am not* always *in the kitchen.* He put a paw on the doorknob and threw open the door. "Yes?"

Skunk—his paw on the door's opposing knob—flew into the room, along with a spatula that flipped free and a whisk that whistled by Badger's ear.

4

Skunk caught himself with a grin. "You *are* here. I knew it! Funny how I flew. Ha!"

Badger observed the smudged and spattered kitchen apron and the wild zag in Skunk's stripe. He spoke with emphasis: "The door was *shut.*" Badger swept a paw in the direction of his rock table (tools out, notebook shoved to one side, an unidentified object bathed in a pool of light). "Important Rock Work?"

Skunk groaned. "This again? You think a closed door is so simple to understand. But as I have explained before, a closed rock room door means more than one possible scenario. Scenario One: You are working on Important Rock Work. In Scenario One, doors must not be knocked upon or opened unexpectedly— not even when lunch is on plates and cooling rapidly. Then there is Scenario Two: You go out for a paw pie at the Veg & Egger. You are not here, but your rock room door is shut." Skunk crossed his arms. "Badger, it is not easy to tell the difference between Scenario One and Scenario Two. If you do not like knocking, you should clarify this situation."

Badger shifted. "Lunch? Left out? To grow cold?"

But Skunk's attention had been captured elsewhere. "Look at those rocks!" Skunk bounded to the windowless wall. He stuck his head near a shelf and squinted up. "One light—one rock, one light–one rock, one light–one rock." He nodded back at Badger. "Clever–that is why the rocks glow."

Badger himself glowed.

Skunk read the name cards. "Neptunite . . . Ob-sid-ian . . . Pyrite . . ." Then Skunk stepped back and tapped his chin. "Alphabetical! You have arranged the rocks in alphabetical order."

Badger nodded happily. "Rocks displayed alphabetically are so satisfactory. I call it . . ." Badger paused for effect. "My Wall of Rocks."

"Wall of Rocks–nice! The chickens will like your Wall of Rocks," said Skunk.

Badger blinked. "Chickens in my rock room? Again?" Badger remembered with horror the last time chickens had been in his rock room. *Chicken coop d'état!* But then he thought of the tiny orange hen no bigger than a pencil mug. *Hm.* He might show Tiny Orange Hen his Wall of Rocks.

Skunk pointed at the empty stand. "Where is *A*?"

*No, no, no,* Badger thought. He purposefully did not look.

Skunk took several steps toward the Wall of Rocks and pointed again. "See Badger? Right here are missing the letter *A* rock. It is fine to arrange rocks alphabetically, but where is *A*?"

Forced, Badger looked. The sight of the empty stand sliced through him. He cleared his throat. "Oh, that. Yes. That is for *Agate*. The, ah, agate was taken." Badger swallowed as he remembered it. Whirls and eyes! Dark, hidden depths! As big as a clenched paw! Badger recalled its coolness when he held it. He used to gaze into it and imagine the birth of Planet Earth. He looked at Skunk. "I called it my Spider Eye Agate."

Skunk frowned. "Are you saying the letter *A* rock is *gone*?"

"Stolen, filched, purloined—yes," Badger whispered.

"That is too bad," said Skunk. He paused, then leaned forward and gave Badger a serious look. "Badger, just put an agate up there. Beginnings are important. You cannot leave a hole at the beginning of your Wall of Rocks."

Badger gulped. "Replace my Spider Eye Agate?"

Skunk's eyes widened. "There is only one letter *A* rock?"

Badger gave a slight nod.

Skunk gaped, then ignited. "There is more than one right letter *A* rock just like there is more than one right way to roast a cauliflower. Why are there so many bossy cookbooks telling one right way to cook?"

Badger stopped listening—as much as Badger liked to eat (and eat a lot), how food got to his plate was of zero interest. Instead, the memory of how he had lost his Spider Eye Agate

7

plowed through him: Aunt Lula's Big House. The Weasel Family Reunion. The Spider Eye Agate not on his nightstand. *Where is it? Where is it?* Everything upturned (shoving aside, shaking out, sorting, sorting, sorting). Then Badger heard *that* voice: "Looking for this?"

Badger had turned and seen his cousin, Fisher, standing in the doorway. Fisher held Badger's Spider Eye Agate in the palm of his paw. Casually, Fisher tossed the agate into the air . . . and caught it. The rock made a smacking sound as it landed in Fisher's paw. Toss, *smack.* Toss, *smack.* Badger's heart leapt with every toss, and (*smack*) felt relief with every catch. "Give it back please," Badger said as calmly as he could manage. He put his paw out.

Toss, *smack.* Fisher smiled, dropped the agate into the pocket of his school blazer, and raised an eyebrow. "Finders keepers," he said.

Aunt Lula, Badger's favorite aunt, had not understood why Badger had to leave the Weasel Family Reunion early. "You'releavingbecauseofarock? Whataboutyourfamily?"

*Fisher!* Badger thought.

(Or thought he thought.)

"What did you say?" said Skunk.

*Had he spoken out loud?* "Nothing, nothing," Badger said.

8

Skunk narrowed his eyes. "It sounded like 'fish.' I would not eat a fish like I would not eat you."

Badger's head spun. He thought, *I might eat a fish.*

Skunk waited.

Badger had the vague idea he was supposed to apologize to fish. He changed the subject. "You knocked? Was there something you wanted?"

"Oh yes! Nearly forgot! Funding–I need currency, coins, paper money." Skunk looked at Badger expectantly. "Yaks will not take muffins. I tried."

"Money for *yaks*?"

"Not for yaks. For a subscription to the Sunday *New Yak Times*. The situation is no longer tolerable." Skunk nodded as if the matter were decided.

Badger opened his mouth to protest, but Skunk spoke quickly. "Every Sunday I go to Chicken Books for the Sunday *New Yak Times*, and yet there have been troubles! One time, Chicken Books ran out of Sunday newspapers! Another time, I got a copy of the Sunday *New Yak Times*, but where is the *Book Review*? It is not in the folds! I toss section after section aside searching, and what is the point of the Sunday *New Yak Times* without the *Book Review*? The *New Yak Times Book Review* is the best part!" Skunk looked at Badger, his foot tapping rapidly. "There is no choice.

We must subscribe." He paused, then muttered, "I do not know why yaks will not take muffins. The best payment is a delicious payment. Everyone knows this."

Badger sighed and glanced with longing at the object on his rock table. The red phenocrysts sparkled enticingly. The first question, rock or mineral, remained unasked! He got to the point. "How much do you need?"

Skunk told him.

Badger readily agreed.

"I am glad that is settled," said Skunk. He grinned at Badger. "You will like the *New Yak Times Book Review* too. Yaks make the best book reviewers. Is it their shaggy bangs that bring focus? Or is it the hump of nutrients, which allows them to read many books without eating? It is a mystery."

Then, with a spring and a skip, Skunk was at the door. He picked up his whisk, then his spatula, off the floor. "Thin and flippy—more useful than you would think," he said, flexing the spatula. He pocketed both of them in his apron. "I need to water Rocket Potato. Have I mentioned how much Rocket Potato is enjoying the pot on the back porch?" (Rocket Potato was a small potato that had once rocketed from a bowl. Skunk and Badger had planted it.) Skunk did not wait for a reply. He looked at

Badger. "Lunch is at noon—*exactly* at noon." Without another word, Skunk leapt out.

Badger's stomach gurgled. The clock read 11:08, fifty-two minutes to lunch.

*Important Rock Work!* Badger thought briskly. He walked to his rock table and picked up the unidentified object. "Rock or mineral?"

He turned the object over in his paws, and raised his voice: "Mineral or rock? Rock? Mineral?"

Then he threw the object into the air.

It went up.

It came down.

It landed in his paw. "ROCK!" Badger yelled.

# CHAPTER TWO

LUNCH? BADGER HESITATED, THEN STUCK HIS HEAD through the kitchen doorway.

Skunk stood at the stove, his apron pocket stuffed with envelopes. The vent hood whooshed. On the stove's burners, two pans sizzled and a pot burbled. Skunk appeared to be cooking lunch and sorting United Pelican mail at the same time. Badger watched Skunk remove an envelope from his apron pocket with one paw while shaking a pan of walnuts with the other. *Chahga. Chahga-chahga.* Skunk read the envelope. "Junk," he muttered. He frisbeed the unopened envelope onto the counter.

"Bock!"

Badger looked and saw a Ko Shamo chicken eyeing the unopened envelope (left eye, tilt-tilt, right eye). Two more chickens (a Silkie and an Orloff) napped nearby, beaks under wings. The Ko Shamo gave the envelope a sharp kick, then fluffed and settled. Badger scanned the kitchen. *No Tiny Orange Hen.*

Skunk grimaced in the Ko Shamo's direction ("Sorry—not paying attention!") and shook the pan of walnuts. *Chahga-chahga-chahga.* The burner's blue flame sparked yellow, red, orange. In the other pan, splotches of batter browned. Steam rose from the pot. The scent of hot apples, honey, and cardamom drifted across Badger's snout.

Badger cleared his throat. "Soon?"

Skunk looked up. He glanced at the wall clock, and then shot Badger a stern look. "Ten minutes."

When Badger failed to move, Skunk grabbed a postcard from the pile of mail on the counter and shoved it at Badger. "Here. Read this." He pointed at Badger's seat at the kitchen table. "Sit."

*Ten minutes?* Badger felt weak in the knees, light in the head. But declarations of hunger did not make food appear faster. (This had been tried.) So Badger nodded feebly and sat in his seat at the kitchen table and picked up the postcard. It was from Aunt Lula. Badger read:

*Greetings Badger & Skunk! I write you from a hemlock forest. The air! The views! The endless opportunities for tree scrambling! I sleep best in trees. Have you tried it? HIGHLY RECOMMEND. —Aunt Lula*

Badger's stomach began to percolate percussively. *Soon,* he told his stomach. He closed his eyes and inhaled. *Onions and . . . zucchini? Yes.* He imagined a plate of zucchini pancakes with . . . ? He sniff-sniffed. *Applesauce! And?* He remembered the small pan. *Toasted walnuts.* Then Badger caught scent of something else . . . *metal, mica, old plumbing pipe.*

*Plumbing pipe?* Badger glanced at Skunk.

And looked again. *Wait. One. Minute.*

If you cooked on a stove, shouldn't you face the stove? In any event, reading a letter and scratching your leg with a spatula while something hissed in a frying pan behind you did not seem like a good idea.

The Silkie flapped. "B-bock!" The Ko Shamo extended her neck. The Orloff sounded alarm: "Brrrrrr-bock-bock-bock!"

Badger's eyes darted to the stove. Smoke rings lifted from the large frying pan.

Then the pan went *poof.* A flame leapt. *Like a solar flare!*

"Flare!" yelled Badger, pointing at the pan.

"Oh!" said Skunk. He smashed the letter and envelope into his apron pocket and spun around. "You should have said something." In a spatula *flick-flick-flick,* the splotches of batter splashed into the sink. The batter splotches weren't the only things lost. "Gone gummy," Skunk said of the contents in the pot. He shook his head at the walnuts in the small frying pan. "Soot and char!"

Sighing, Skunk clunked the pot and two pans into the sink and looked at the chickens. "Lunch another time?" One by one, the chickens step-step-stepped to the sink, eyed the pans and pot (left eye, right eye, left eye), and flap-fluttered off the counter. "B-bock-bock-bock." Skunk escorted them out the back door and called, "Yes! Another time!" Then Skunk returned to the kitchen. He gave the air a sniff and turned off the vent hood. With a whoosh, silence fell.

Skunk turned and faced Badger. "I got the worst letter. Read it now, please." He pulled the smashed envelope and letter from his apron pocket and held them out.

Badger took them. On the envelope, the return address read:

Mr. G. Hedgehog
North Twist

It was addressed to:

Mr. Skunk
Ms. Lula P. Marten's Brownstone
North Twist

Badger smoothed out the stationery and read:

Mr. Skunk,

I have recently relocated to North Twist. I understand you also live in North Twist now. I am writing to inform you that I would like to continue our previous arrangement. I'll be by on Sunday morning for the *New Yak Times Book Review*.

I was sorry to hear about the confrontation with the Speedy Stoat Delivery stoat. The clientele at Chicken Books discussed it for many days. Of course, I knew of your involvement. The scent signature was unmistakably yours.

Most obliged,

Mr. G. Hedgehog


This did not seem like "the worst letter" to Badger. He looked up, unsure of what to say.

"See? See?" Skunk hop-hopped and gestured at the letter. He nodded as if Badger did indeed see.

"Ah . . ." Badger managed.

Skunk clarified: "If Mr. G. Hedgehog is in North Twist, he will take my *Book Review*!"

Badger frowned. "Take? That's not what he says." Badger scanned the letter, then tapped the line. "He mentions a 'previous arrangement.'"

Skunk gasped. "Previous arrangement? There is no previous arrangement. It is the *New Yak Times Book Review*! The only arrangement is this: I lay the *Book Review* on the kitchen table, eat a muffin, and read. *That* is the arrangement." Skunk threw his paws into the air and began to pace. "Mr. G. Hedgehog—of all hedgehogs! Why is he here?"

Skunk nodded at Badger. "I know Mr. G. Hedgehog from the place I lived before. I subscribed to the Sunday *New Yak*

*Times*, and within two weeks—two weeks!—the *Book Review* went missing."

Skunk stopped to look at Badger. "I tried everything! At first, I thought I could grab the newspaper as soon as it hit the pavement. (It is unfortunate I am a good sleeper.) Then I arranged for the newspaper to be left in a high, out-of-the-way 'Peaches in Syrup' can. Foiled! After that I put water sprinklers on trip wires. Why was I the only one to get wet?" Skunk paced. "Now Mr. G. Hedgehog has arrived in North Twist! What can be done? Once again, I will find the *Book Review* crumpled beneath a rhododendron bush. Or shoved beneath juice bottles in the recycle bin. Or rolled into a discarded, toeless boot."

*Surely this wasn't so difficult!* Badger said slowly, "Perhaps you should discuss the situation with Mr. G. Hedgehog. If you told him—"

Skunk held up a paw. "There is no talking to a hedgehog like that!"

This did not sound like trying everything, but Badger did not say so.

A lost look appeared on Skunk's face. "How will I decide what to read on Long Story Night? No *Book Review* is a big loss. Think, think, think."

Badger's stomach gave a pop. He glanced at the clock and saw the clock's big hand and little hand united, joined gloriously at the number twelve. *Noon!* Badger shook out his napkin—*flip, flip, flip*—and laid it in his lap. He gripped his fork and waited, fork in paw.

Skunk observed Badger. He looked at the dishes in the sink, glanced back at Badger, then went to the cupboards. He crossed the room with a box of cereal and set it in front of Badger. A bowl and spoon were clunked next to it, followed by a glass of water (which sloshed).

Badger stared at the cereal box. *This is unexpected.* He laid down his fork.

Skunk looked at Badger. "Lunch is ruined. Pans are dirty. You like cereal." With a nod, Skunk returned to the sink. He squeezed dish soap into it and turned on the faucet. Then he picked up a pan and began to scrub. *Ratcha-ratcha-ratch.*

Badger swallowed one spoonful of watery cereal.

"*X* marks the spot!" The pan splashed into the sink. Skunk leapt into the air. "Rock-finding expedition!"

Badger nearly fell from his chair.

Skunk slid across the floor. "Picnic every day. Sleep under the stars. Cook on a fire." Skunk nodded. "You need an *A* agate for your Wall of Rocks. I do not want to be at home on

Sunday. What is a Sunday without the *Book Review*? But a rock-finding expedition would be another thing altogether. That is an adventure. I will provide provisions!" Skunk snatched the cereal box off the table. "Done with this?" He looked at Badger. "Time to get packing. We leave on Thursday."

"Hang on, hang on!" Badger grabbed the cereal box and set it firmly on the kitchen table. "I have Important Rock Work."

"Fine. We leave on Friday then," said Skunk, as if they'd settled on a compromise. He leaned forward. "How far away is this agate? How many days are required? Planning is required for provisions."

"No planning. No provisions. Let me think!" Badger shooed Skunk through the pocket doors into the living room. (This room was Badger's former rock room. It had been recently rearranged to include a couch, two wing-backed chairs, and cases filled with books and board games.)

Skunk threw himself on the couch. "You should say 'yes'!"

Badger turned his chair so he wouldn't have to look at Skunk's propped-up feet.

A rock-finding expedition? Impossible! Badger had not studied his geological survey maps. He had not drawn diagrams and sketches of rocks in layers: Folding! Faulting! The expected intrusions!

*But agates.* Endless Lake, the place he had found his Spider Eye Agate, was only a half day's walk away. He could set up his tent at his favorite campsite–Campsite #5. How long did he intend to pine for his lost Spider Eye Agate? Skunk was right. Enough was enough. Replace the agate. Put Fisher and his treachery firmly in the past.

Also, if Skunk went along, the food situation would vastly improve.

"One Sunday. We will be gone one week only," Badger said with a low growl.

Skunk leapt from the couch and approached with a gallop.

Badger held up a paw.

Skunk skidded to a halt.

"It doesn't solve your problem with the hedgehog–not if you want to read the *Book Review*," said Badger.

Skunk tapped his chin. "I see what you mean." Then Skunk grinned widely. "But that will be a problem for next Sunday. This Sunday, at least, I will not have to face a Sunday *New Yak Times* without its *Book Review*. In the meantime: Cook on a fire. Sleep under the stars. Picnic every day. *X* marks the spot! *X, X, X!*"

Badger couldn't help himself–he smiled. "You provide the food."

Skunk gave him a serious look. "And you provide the *X*."

"Agreed." Badger stuck out a paw.

Skunk hesitated. "Will you mark the spot with an *X*? I would like it if you did."

"No," said Badger.

Skunk shrugged. "I can live with that." Then Skunk took Badger's paw and shook it.

This was Tuesday.

# CHAPTER THREE

AT BREAKFAST ON WEDNESDAY, SKUNK SET A MUG OF HOT chocolate in front of Badger and said, "Do you need a pencil and paper for planning? I can spare one eraser too. I find it easier to plan with an eraser nearby. You cannot spend all your time sleeping, Badger. Gear and provisions must be gathered. I recommend a chart." Skunk waved a chart in front of Badger's face.

Badger batted away the paper and slugged back his breakfast hot chocolate.

With a *harrumph*, Skunk returned to the stove. There was a sizzle as a tortilla was dropped into a pan. In another pan, an egg was *k-crack*ed. *SSSss!* Badger's stomach yowled. He spied muffins cooling on a rack. Badger stood and reached.

Skunk leapt in front of Badger's paw. "Sit down! Those are my trading muffins. Your breakfast is coming!"

With a whimper, Badger sat.

After an "mmm," a spatula scrape, and a "yes, yes, yes," Skunk crossed the room with a rimmed plate. "Huevos Motuleños! One of the best breakfasts ever invented." A fried egg and a tostada balanced on a black bean island. The island rose out of a red sea. (Cinnamon! Chilies! Roasted tomatoes!) Fresh peas and fried plantains bobbled at the island's edges. Badger did not hesitate. He picked up his spoon and marooned himself on that eggy island.

When Badger looked up again, he found himself alone.

"Hup, hup," he said. It was time to get out his rock-expedition checklist. Badger did the dishes and then charged up the stairs. *To the file cabinet!*

————◄○►————

At noon, a large yellow backpack sat in the front hallway. Badger jogged over to examine it. External frame. *Extremely adjustable.* Thick straps with brass buckles held the lid in place. Two water bottle pockets, an ice ax loop, *and* a pocket in the lid flap! He rubbed a claw over the label and let out a low whistle. The backpack was paw-crafted and paw-sewn by the badger geniuses at SunSett Adventures—a backpack made by badgers *for* badgers.

*Huh*, Badger thought.

Badger found Skunk in the kitchen with an Orpington. Skunk sat at the table twirling a pencil in his claws. The chicken stood on the tabletop. They studied Skunk's chart. The Orpington right-eyed the chart, left-eyed the chart, then tilted her head in Skunk's direction. "Bock, bock-bock." She pecked the chart. The paper jumped.

"Excuse me." Badger gestured toward the hallway. "That backpack—"

"Badger! Good!" Skunk jabbed the air with the pencil. "Do you have plates, cups, and two sporks? I need your equipment list. Also, you said you had an extra sleeping bag. I will use it."

"Sleeping bag. Equipment list. Got it. Now about that backpack in the hallway . . ." Badger paused as his eyes snagged on the sight of a cast-iron frying pan and a cast-iron stewpot. Neither had been in the kitchen earlier. *Cast iron? Isn't cast iron heavy?* A hefty fire grate leaned against cabinetry. It looked weighty.

He felt eyes upon him, and found Skunk and the Orpington (left eye, right eye, blink) watching.

Badger got to the point. "Skunk, is that *your* yellow backpack? The *big* one? In the hallway?"

Skunk nodded. "Innes, at the Veg & Egger, said I could have it. She said, 'Skunk, take it off my paws. All it does is take up space!' Her idea of a vacation is a view, a bed, and a good book."

Badger blurted, "Innes is an American *badger*. Skunk, that is a *big* backpack."

"The bigger the better! Who needs a small backpack?" Skunk's eyes flashed. "*And* it is yellow! With three pockets! It is perfect."

"You put it on?"

"Oh yes! It is the best backpack ever."

Badger gaped open-mouthed and decided it was none of his business.

———◄◌►———

On Thursday, Badger laid out everything he planned to take on the floor of his rock room and began paring down the weight of his load. If the item was needed, he would take it. Multiple uses would further reduce the number of items. Finally, he would whittle away weight. "No one needs the handle on a toothbrush!" *Snap!*

Needed: his Go-Burrow tent with tent fly, poles, and stakes. Also needed: his Lava Bed sleeping bag with orange interior and repeating volcano-and-lava-field exterior. And he was taking the sleeping pad! Without a good night's sleep what use would he be? Badger preferred objects made with titanium (*Strong and light!*) and silicone (*Light and squashy!*). He felt genuine affection for aluminum (*Light!*) but thought it a risk. (*A shame it is so fragile.*)

The remaining items were interrogated. "Prove your worth!" Badger growled. "Why are you necessary? How many tasks do you do? More than one? Two? Three?" If the item passed, Badger dropped it on the scale and weighed it. Badger kept the bandana. (Napkin, potholder, hat. Weight? 0.5 ounces.) He considered the benefits of the X34 Mighty Blaze flashlight. (*Unnecessary! I can see in the dark!* Followed by: *It only weighs two ounces! Extra illumination is helpful.*) He decided to take the flashlight and leave his comb. (*What are claws for?*) Then Badger packed his Heave Ho Hauler backpack to see if everything fit.

Badger tugged over the lid and buckled it down. *It fits! But can I carry it?* With a *harrumph*, Badger threaded himself through the straps, clasped the hip belt and sternum strap, cinched them tight, and leaned forward. Contents shifted. The canvas moaned. He took one step, two steps . . . In a burst, Badger squatted down, stood up, hopped on one hind foot, hopped on the other, and clapped his paws. "YES!" His Heave Ho Hauler might be dinged, scratched, and bent, but it had proven its worth time and time again. "Good ol' Heave Ho." To celebrate, Badger freed himself from the pack and picked up his ukulele. A rock-finding expedition *without* a ukulele? What was the point? A ukulele was necessary!

Now, Badger ran his claws across the strings. *Beed . . . el . . . lee . . . boNG.*

Badger grimaced and turned the string's tuner while repeatedly plucking. *BoNG . . . bung . . . bang . . . bing.*

With a nod, he strummed. *Beed-el-lee-bing!*

A song followed. "Eons" was a song Badger had written himself. It was about Earth's history in big chunks of time. The time chunks were called *eons. Tuneful and of Geological Import!*

Badger closed his eyes and began with a howl ("AaaaaaooooOOOH") and a rattling C7 strum.

The song went like this:

**BIG (D7!) BA-BOOM (D7!) BANG (D7!)**

(D7) Hadean eon

> *Happy birthday, Earth! Volcanos. Seas of acid. Watch out for meteorites.*

(E7) Archean eon

*The Rock Record begins. Bacteria, bacteria, bacteria at last!*

(F7) Proterozoic eon

*Worms, jellyfish, and Snowball Earth. Worms, jellyfish, and Snowball Earth.*

(G7) Phanerozoic eon

*Look, shells! Have you ever seen shells before? No!*

*Life evolves, diversifies, explosion—BANG (G7!)—of life.*

*Age of Dinosaurs—meteorite CRASH (G7!)—Age of Mammals.*

A strolling A chord, G chord, D chord concluded the verse, giving Badger time to mentally prepare for the second verse. The second verse broke the Phanerozoic eon into eras and periods. The "explosion of life" had been extensive. Endurance was required.

Another C7 rattling strum! Badger sucked in air, opened his mouth to sing, and—

"Is that a song?" Badger heard.

Badger opened his eyes. There stood Skunk. In his rock room. Again.

Skunk saw the look on Badger's face and gestured at the door. "You still do not have a sign. You were not yelling ROCK or MINERAL. Also, I heard the ukulele." He leaned forward. "Who is Ian?"

Badger moaned. "Eon—not Ian. A division of geological time?"

"Oh. Okay." Skunk scratched an ear, then looked into the jumbled part of the attic. "That bathtub has something I would like for our rock-finding expedition. Do you mind?"

Badger did not.

Skunk disappeared into the bathtub. He reappeared with a tricornered hat.

Badger blinked.

Skunk flexed the hat. "Three corners! Not every hat comes with *three* corners." Skunk tucked the tricornered hat under an elbow and left.

————◄◊►————

Friday morning began with a *ba-BOOM!* and a flash of lightning. Badger brought his packed Heave Ho Hauler down to the back porch and leaned it against the brownstone.

The rain beat down. *Putta-putta-putta.*

Skunk followed Badger out. He carried two bowls of peanut butter and banana oatmeal. He handed Badger one of the bowls and a spoon and began eating from the other.

*The rain beat down.* Putta-putta-putta.

Badger swallowed a spoonful and said, "As soon as the rain breaks, we'll head out." He felt a surge of joy. *Endless Lake! A rock-finding expedition!* It had been far too long. Why had he delayed?

*K-k-k-BOOM! Putta-putta-put-put.*

Badger looked at Skunk. "You all ready to go?"

Skunk nodded. "Nearly." He grinned at Badger. "The chickens were so much help with my packing list. A chicken notices everything–peck and hunt, hunt and peck. I can honestly say I have considered every eventuality, outcome, alteration, revision, and modification. And all weather conditions."

Badger grunted assent and ate more oatmeal.

"The minute you think you know a chicken, you are in for a surprise!" Skunk looked at Badger. "Ha! Chickens and physics was a big shock to you. Ha-ha!"

Badger did not find this amusing.

Skunk waited.

Badger huffed. "Fine. Yes. The chickens are *surprisingly* conversant with physics."

"Conversant? Ha! How can you say chickens are only 'conversant with' physics? The chickens utilize the Quantum Leap, disappearing in one spot and reappearing in another. That is impressive!" Skunk paused and tapped his foot. "I did not care for henhouse living, however. Skunks are not made for roosting." Skunk raised his eyebrows and sighed. "It is pleasant eating oatmeal on a porch while it is raining, but shall we? I have a few final preparations to make and then I will be ready to go." Skunk went inside. The screen door slammed behind him.

*Putta-putta-putta.*

Badger gulped the last of his oatmeal, stepped to the edge of the porch, and peered into the bruised sky. Then he went inside too.

*A few final preparations?* Skunk's "preparations" covered chairs, countertops, the kitchen table. Bags and baggies bulged. Prepacked lunch sacks lined the kitchen counter. Cooking utensils were stockpiled in crocks. A muddle of camping gear crammed the corner. Bags of dried fruit (raisins, apricots, apple slices) were heaped in the cast-iron frying pan. Onions, potatoes, and carrots filled the stewpot. Badger saw a five-pound bag of flour. (*Five pounds?*) The tricornered hat teetered jauntily on a hefty Blue Hubbard squash. Where were the items made of titanium and silicone? He'd settle for some aluminum! Badger searched in vain. It was not there. *Too much. Too many. Too heavy!*

Badger set his oatmeal bowl on top of a prepacked lunch (there was nowhere else) and cleared his throat. "Does all of this fit? Have you tried packing it? We are leaving as soon as the weather clears."

Skunk seemed surprised. "I always pack my red suitcase right before I leave."

Badger gestured around. "But Skunk, there is more here than pajamas, a chicken whistle, and your storybook."

Skunk considered this and said, "I *am* taking my pajamas and the chicken whistle, but I am not taking the storybook."

Badger could not think about it. He waved a paw. "Find me when you're packed. I'll be in my rock room."

The kitchen looked no better at lunch. ("I thought we should use up our old bread. French onion soup with croutons.")

Or at dinner. ("The last of the old bread–peach bread pudding! Also: coconut rice with roasted vegetables.")

Anyway–*Putta-putta-put*–it was still raining.

Over dinner, Skunk agreed they should leave on Saturday morning.

"First thing?" Badger asked, in pain as he glanced at the piles still piled around him.

Skunk nodded vigorously. "The *New Yak Times Book Review* comes on Sunday. I do not want to get any closer to Sunday than is absolutely necessary."

On Saturday, Badger expected the worst. With a heavy heart, he descended the stairs.

Behold, the yellow SunSett Adventures backpack! Packed and upright! The kitchen was uncluttered and clean. A candle was lit on the kitchen table. Two places were set with place mats, napkins, eating utensils, and a glass of water. Badger did a slow turn and then sat down. "It's all packed?"

"Yup!" Skunk clunked down a mug of breakfast hot chocolate and a plate filled with an egg and avocado sandwich, and started in, full of news: "Everything fits—everything! It was touch and go for a while." Skunk grinned. "What a backpack! We will not have to do without during picnics." Skunk patted it as he flitted past, carrying his own mug and plate. He sat down across from Badger.

The glimpse of Skunk next to the backpack halted Badger mid-chew. *Yellow makes everything appear larger,* he told himself. Still, the pack loomed. It towered and eclipsed. Badger swallowed hard and observed the lumps and bulges, the stretched canvas. Why the right angles? Why were thoughts of fire pokers, potato mashers, and scissors dancing in his head? Badger set his sandwich on his plate.

Skunk's head bounced cheerfully back and forth as he chewed.

"Have you, ah, tried putting the backpack on now that it's packed?" Badger asked.

Skunk gave Badger a look. "Why? It is a *pack* for your *back*. If it can be *packed*, it can be *backed*. So to speak." He frowned. "What do you think a backpack does?"

"Huh," Badger managed to squeak.

They did the dishes together. Skunk handed Badger the last dish, dried his paws on his sweater, and said, "Time to get your backpack. We leave in five minutes!"

Badger's Heave Ho Hauler was up in his bedroom. He paused and shot Skunk a pained look. "Need any assistance with that pack?" He tried for a casual smile.

Skunk pulled a face. "Nah, I got it."

Badger took the stairs two at a time. It was as he opened the door to his bedroom that he heard it:

"AhHH!"

*ThhhhhhhhhhWHACK!*

Badger raced down the stairs and into the kitchen.

In the middle of the floor was Skunk, strapped to the backpack, arms and legs waving. "Oh there you are Badger. Would you mind giving me a paw up, please?"

# CHAPTER FOUR

"YOU'LL HAVE TO TAKE SOME OF IT OUT," BADGER SAID.

Skunk shook his head. "That is not possible. What is in, is in."

Badger rubbed his brow. "Skunk, you fell over."

"I lost my balance." Skunk looked around the kitchen. He pointed. "Help me get the backpack on that chair."

After much grappling, heaving, and grunting, they'd done it. The yellow backpack rested on the seat of the chair. Now Skunk leaned a shoulder into the pack. One of his hind feet braced the chair leg. He huffed in and out.

Badger reached to help.

"NO." Skunk shot him a steely look, then huff-huffed for air. "Get your backpack ON." (Another huff.) "WAIT for me . . ." (Huff-huff.) ". . . in the HALLWAY." (Huff.)

◄◇►

Two minutes later and backpack on, Badger stood in the front hallway. He heard muttering coming from the kitchen: "Yes." (Huff.) "Okay." (Huff.) "Okay-okay-okay." (Huff.) Canvas creaked. Contents clanked. And then: "UNGH." The chair screeched and hit the floor. *CLAP!*

Badger waited for the howl that was sure to follow.

Instead, an enormous yellow backpack tottered into the hallway on two tiny legs. "DOOR . . . OPEN . . . PLEASE."

Badger backed into the front door and twisted around to open it. "Don't forget the steps to the sidewalk," Badger called as the yellow backpack turned sideways to make its way down the front steps. It teetered down (step-together), down (step-together), and down (step-together). "Right at the bottom," Badger called as he locked the brownstone.

The yellow backpack made the right and moved steadily forward.

*Trudge. Trudge. Trudge.*

Two yard sheep, chewing in circles, watched the yellow backpack pass and then stared at Badger as he raced after it.

"Staring is rude," Badger hissed.

"Blaaaa," said a yard sheep unblinkingly.

Beside the yellow backpack, Badger said, "I've got the map. I'll lead, all right?"

Skunk's voice floated up. "Okay."

*Trudge. Trudge. Trudge.*

Badger stepped into the path. "Are you *sure* you can see me from under that backpack?"

"Your ankles (*trudge*) . . . are right there (*trudge*) . . . Keep moving!" (*Trudge.*)

So Badger led. The yellow backpack followed. Badger's ears became tuned to: *Trudge. Trudge.* If Badger did not hear the expected *trudge*, he whipped around in alarm, full of worry.

This was hardly the trip to Endless Lake Badger had imagined. Worse, it could have been the perfect walk! Friday's storm had left a world tossed and dazzling in emeralds, jades, and turquoise. The sun shone. Two clouds drifted across a blue sky. Skunk should have been shouting hellos to the goats in that field. And that knotted apple tree? Skunk should have picked an apple. *Tannin, tannin, tannin—very puckery*, Badger imagined Skunk saying. *I would call it a "cider apple." What would you call it, Badger?*

But none of this happened.

What happened was: *Trudge. Trudge. Trudge.*

It was like being tracked by a looming cheese!

By the time Badger reached Accordion Ridge, Skunk had been *trudge-trudge-trudging* for four hours. *Four hours!* In addition, Accordion Ridge was the highest point and less than a mile away from Campsite #5 at Endless Lake. Skunk had nearly done it! Badger turned to watch the yellow backpack make the ascent. When it reached him, Badger told Skunk firmly that it was time to eat.

With a *trudge*, the yellow backpack stopped. Skunk's knees shuddered. The strap's buckles began to rattle, and then the load leaned. Badger hastily backed the yellow backpack onto a boulder and freed Skunk from its straps.

Sweaty, soaked through, Skunk looked half-drowned. There was a vague, faraway look in Skunk's eyes as he fumbled with the buckles on the yellow backpack and finally flung a lunch sack weakly in Badger's direction. (It landed in ferns.) Then Skunk clutched his water bottle, unscrewed the cap, and *ga-ga-ga-ga-ga-ga*-guzzled.

Badger took his lunch sack to a grassy spot with a view of the valley. Skunk plunked down next to Badger and opened his own lunch sack with a heavy sigh. He pulled out the sandwich, unwrapped it one parchment corner at a time, and took a bite. Mid-sandwich-chew, his head bobbed, then wobbled. With a grunt, his head fell (along with the sandwich). "Thuuuugnnnnnng . . . ggh . . . gah."

"Skunk?" Badger shook his shoulder.

Skunk's eyes popped open. "Nice meadow . . . Big view . . . North Twist is so small."

"I'm carrying that backpack," Badger said forcefully. "You've carried it enough."

Skunk turned to gaze at the yellow backpack, then twisted back around and stared out at the view.

So Badger did the same. In rocky (*basalt!*) pleats, Accordion Ridge dropped into blue-green hills. Hill after hill continued, until there it was—a spattering of roofs, a spire, a line of brownstones.

"I like it here," said Skunk.

Badger smiled and shook out his map. "Let me show you where we are."

Skunk leaned to look and took another bite of sandwich.

They sat like that for a while, with Skunk finishing his lunch and Badger pointing things out on his map. When Skunk started asking questions ("Is that Endless Lake?" "Where is Campsite Number Five?") Badger knew Skunk felt more like himself.

In the end, Skunk refused to let Badger carry the yellow backpack. "Only a half an hour and all downhill? Downhill is the easiest part!" Badger tried to suggest that downhill was often trickier than uphill, but Skunk was having none of it. "I walked all the way up here. I am nearly there," he said as Badger helped him strap on the yellow backpack.

*Trudge. Trudge. Trudge.*

Badger watched Skunk mount the last few feet of hill and disappear around a bend. Then he went for his Heave Ho Hauler.

"Whoa!" The yell stopped Badger in his tracks.

Branches creaked. He heard a skittering. "Whoa-whoa!"

And then: *WHUMP!* Something smacked down hard.

"WhOOOOooooaaaaaaAAAAH!"

"Skunk!" Badger took off at a run, slinging on his Heave Ho Hauler as he went.

———◄○►———

Badger saw snapped twigs. And a flattened sapling tree.

Around the first turn, he found a ladle. A few steps later? A cast-iron frying pan.

At the top of a steep rise, a bellows teetered.

"No!" Badger stepped to the crest and looked down.

Down . . . down . . . down the slope Badger saw a splash of yellow with a Skunk-sized dot on it.

"Hang on, Skunk! I'm coming!" Badger yelled.

"IS THIS THE WOODS?" he heard.

Skunk was stretched out on top of the yellow backpack, elbows back, his head cradled in his paws. He seemed to be looking at the sky. As Badger approached, Skunk rolled to one side, leaned on his elbow, and said, "Have you ever seen so many leafy islands bobbling out on tree limbs?"

Badger squinted at him. "Are you okay?"

"I am fine? I think?" Skunk sat up, rolled his paws and hind feet, then nodded. "Yes, I am fine."

Badger should have felt relief, but he had thrown himself down the hill with a backpack on. He'd battled gravity, twiggy undergrowth, and uncertain footing. And if that weren't enough, he'd done it while carrying an odd assortment of awkward and heavy items. Badger let everything fall from his arms. The bellows, the ladle, and the cast-iron frying pan clattered to the ground. "What happened back there?"

Skunk shook his head in wonder. "I slipped and then slid down the hill on top of the backpack—like an egg stuck on toast! I do not recommend it. Who would choose to go headfirst and backwards?" Then he shrugged. "It was invigorating. I will say that much for it." He looked around. "So many trees!" Skunk stood up and rubbed a shoulder while slowly turning. "Tree after tree after tree after tree . . . after tree." He looked at Badger. "Are we officially *in* the woods?"

Badger frowned. "I suppose so."

"Ha! I am in the woods! Finally!" Skunk spun on one foot and landed by sitting on the yellow backpack.

Badger peered at Skunk. "You've *never* been in the woods before? But you know how to cook on a fire."

Skunk gave him a look. "You do not have to be in the woods to cook on a fire. I cooked on a number-ten tin-can stove when I lived under the . . ." He looked at Badger and did not finish his thought.

A song threaded its way through the air. It chortled, curled back on itself, then spiraled away.

Skunk sat up straighter. "Elves?"

"Har!" Badger laughed. "A wood thrush is singing."

"Wood thrush," Skunk repeated in a hush. "I must meet a wood thrush." Then he yawned, rubbed his eyes, and yawned again. With a panicked look, he got to his feet and jumped up and down. "Wake up! Wake up!" He looked at Badger with urgency. "How close are we to Campsite Number Five?"

Badger turned around and saw, over to his left, a post with the number 5 burned into it. "Incredible," Badger muttered. He swung his paw out. "Campsite Number Five is right over there. You found the short way down." The campsite was as Badger remembered it. He smiled as he took in the firepit with the sitting log and the mossy spot for his tent.

"Good," said Skunk. He pulled out another sack lunch and shoved it into Badger's paws. "Eat this. I am going to bed NOW."

It was only four o'clock.

Ten minutes later, Badger sat on the pebbly shoreline of Endless Lake eating a peanut butter and jelly sandwich. A ring-billed gull circled. "Ow! ah-Wow. Ow! ah-Wow. Ow, ow, ow." Water wa*shhhed*-wa*shhhed*-wa*shhhed*.

Badger took a bite of his sandwich and remembered. *Endless Lake—where it all began!* He'd had a traditional badger upbringing in a claw-dug sett under a tree. It was cozy, but dark and tunneled, with one too many siblings (four). As a kit, Badger often escaped the den's tumbles and tussles at Endless Lake. This was where he had skipped a stone twenty-three times!

Badger picked up one of the blue-gray skipping stones now and rolled it in his paw. *Old basalt. Precambrian.* Back then, Badger hadn't known that his favorite skipping stone was lava from an eruption that occurred 1.1 billion years ago. Anyway, searching for skippers had led to rummaging in the rocks and rock rummaging had led to agates.

Badger had found his Spider Eye Agate after a big storm. Storms kicked up ridges of rocks along the shoreline, so Badger had gotten up early to search after the storm broke. That morning, golden light spilled through the loosening thunderheads. The rocks shone with rainwater. He found the agate out in the open, at the top of a ridge. It was as big as a balled-up paw and full of color, swirls, and eyes. He named it his "Spider Eye" because of those eyes—circles within circles (whites, yellows, shades of orange, and reds). It wasn't long before the questions came: How were the eyes formed? Why were some parts of the agate clear and other parts murky? Why the rusty color? And so, question by question, Badger learned rock science.

Yes, his Spider Eye Agate had begun it all.

*Fisher!* Badger heard Fisher's voice in his head: "Finders keepers." Toss, *smack*.

Suddenly, Badger felt winded and hopeless. *What am I doing here? My Spider Eye Agate will always be my letter A*

*rock!* With heaviness, Badger swallowed his last bite of sandwich.

The sun was setting. On the water, colors stretched and shimmered. A breeze scooted across the water's surface, then tumbled back to etch, erase, and scribble. One wave broke, then another. A slant, a slide, a slip—the *slap, slap, slap* of water on rocks.

"Har!" Badger laughed. Wasn't it enough that his Spider Eye Agate had set him on his way? That agate had done him good, wherever it rested now.

When Badger got back to Campsite #5, Skunk was fast asleep in the middle of the clearing. He lay in his pajamas on top of the sleeping bag he'd borrowed from Badger. Badger sniffed the air for rain and decided Skunk would be fine sleeping out in the open.

Then Badger noticed the yellow backpack. *Hm.* He went to inspect it. One of the two straps holding the lid had snapped, but the canvas remained intact. *No holes. Or rips.* Badger ran a paw over the fabric and shook his head. *SunSett Adventures!* You could ride a SunSett Adventures pack down a hill and it remained useable! The yellow backpack was also full of food. It needed to be kept away from other animals. He made a mental note.

After he set up his tent and finished his chores, Badger took out his ukulele.

*Beed-el-lee-bing!* sounded the ukulele.

*Bip! BiddleePEEP!* sang a whip-poor-will.

He strummed again. *Beed-el-lee-bing!*

*Bip! BiddleePEEP! Bip! BiddleePEEP!* the whip-poor-will sang.

*A satisfying day!* Badger thought when he finally crawled into his tent. He shed his layers and fell asleep.

# CHAPTER FIVE

A *THUD* FOLLOWED BY A LESSER *THUD*.

Badger shuddered awake. He tossed on clothing, unzipped the tent fly, and bolted into the clearing with incisors bared.

"GrrrRRRR–OH," he said, stopping abruptly. Both backpacks lay on the ground, a pulley and rope beside them.

"You will not believe it." Skunk marched up. He wore the tricornered hat. "Guess where our backpacks were this morning? You will *never* guess." Skunk did not wait for Badger to guess. He gestured grandly at the big tree at the edge of Campsite #5. "In that tree! High up–*very* high up! Whoever did it used this pulley and that rope. Why would anyone do that? It took me forever to find my backpack and then I looked up. Badger, the last thing I expected to see was my yellow backpack hanging in the air. It is hardly a balloon!"

Badger said, "I did that. I put the backpacks in the tree."

Skunk stared. "Why would you do that?"

Badger explained: "So the bears wouldn't get into them."

Skunk's nose crumpled up. "Because of *bears*?"

"Yes. To keep them out of the food."

"Bears?"

"Better safe than sorry."

"HA!" Skunk folded over: "Ha-ha-ha-ha-HA!" He came halfway up and slapped his knee. "Oh Badger, you had me. BEARS—good one!" He held his sides. "I (ha-ha-ha) almost believed (ha-ha-ha) that bears (ha) were REAL (ha-ha-ha-ha)."

Badger crossed his arms. "Bears *are* real."

"No!" Skunk inhaled sharply. He stared at Badger for a long moment. "Are you saying bears *live* in the woods? Or are you trying to put one over on a city skunk like me?"

Badger answered clearly and with enunciation. "YES. Bears. Live. In the woods."

"Really! Huh." Skunk blinked and looked into the woods around him. Then Skunk nodded. "Okay—bears," he said with a shrug. He looked at Badger. "But what about unicorns? I heard a narwhal speak once, and what is more likely? A dolphin with a horn? Or a horse with a horn?"

———◄◦►———

Breakfast was fresh biscuits (*A five-pound bag of flour?*) and eggs (*In a backpack?*) fried in the cast-iron (*Heavy!*) frying pan. The bellows was kept at the ready to–*Pffft. Pffft. Pffft.*–stoke the fire. And yet, as Badger slugged back the last drops of his fire cocoa, he had to admit it was the best rock-finding expedition breakfast he had ever eaten.

"Bravo!" Badger called.

Skunk swept the tricornered hat off his head and took a bow.

They did the dishes. They tidied the campsite. They packed up the day's knapsacks. Then Badger began the job of stringing the two backpacks into the tree. Skunk stepped between Badger and the yellow SunSett Adventures pack. "Are you *sure* this is necessary? It is very inconvenient."

Badger countered: "A bear will eat *all* the food."

Skunk frowned. "All of it?"

"*All* of it." Badger put his paw on the pack.

Skunk gave him a concerned look but stepped aside. Badger pulleyed the packs up and tied the rope off with a knot.

"ONWARD TO *X*!" yelled Skunk. Badger pointed out the path to Endless Lake. Skunk leapt ahead. Badger clutched his knapsack and jogged after him. At Endless Lake, they walked along the pebbly shoreline. An hour later they came to a creek. They followed the creek into the woods. ("Woods," Skunk whispered.) After fifteen minutes, Badger heard eighth notes, triplets, and syncopated patter. The banks grew sloped. They rounded a leafy bend, and . . . ? The waterfall! The water spooled off the top and poured onto ledge after ledge. It hit the pool below in rat-a-tats, snare drum rolls, and a rainbow-rising *shhhhhhhh!*

Skunk grinned and put his paws on his hips. "This looks like *X*."

"Well, yes. It is *X*—I suppose. This *is* where we were headed."

"*X* MARKS THE SPOT!" Skunk threw off his knapsack and unbuckled the top. A moment later, he was wading into the stream wearing his tricornered hat and carrying a tin plate.

"What are you doing?" asked Badger.

"Panning for agates, of course!" said Skunk. He put a paw into the water and came up with a paw-full of stones. He piled these onto his plate and shook the plate. "Ah!" Skunk plucked a stone from the plate and put it in a pocket.

Badger's eyes took in the waterfall. *Important Rock Work—hup, hup!* He unpacked his knapsack and hung his rock hammer, chisel, and brush on his tool belt. He put the lanyard of his magnifying loupe around his neck. He tied his bandana onto his head. Then Badger spied a rock of interest (*huh*) and went over to investigate (*hm*).

And so, the morning passed.

Lunch was leftover biscuits, three granola bars, and two salty pretzels. While they ate, they compared finds. Skunk poured a paw-full of tiny agates into Badger's paw. Badger sorted them with a claw. "Hmm . . . Yes, yes . . . Huh."

Skunk watched and then said, "This one is my favorite," and pulled a chunk of fine-grained basalt from his pocket. "Look!" He tapped his claw on a striped agate stuck in the basalt.

Badger grinned. "An embedded agate—very nice!"

Then Badger showed Skunk the moss agate he had found ("Are there plants growing in it?") and a hunk of black and red jasper. ("Good colors. So smooth.")

After lunch, Skunk declared nap time. "I will be under that tree over there," he said, pointing.

A nap under a leafy tree sounded inviting but Badger was doing Important Rock Work, and every minute counted. *Focus, focus, focus.*

————◄○►————

Badger was leaning over a pool when he heard footsteps behind him.

"Why hello, Badger."

*That* voice. Badger froze.

"Hunting for agates? Again? Ho-ho!"

Badger flicked water off his claws and turned.

There he stood. Badger took in the straw fedora, the seersucker suit, the walking stick, and the lemon-yellow loafers. "What do you want, Fisher?"

"Is it like that, cousin?" Fisher made a show of wincing. "Oh dear—I thought we were friends."

Badger snorted. "Friends don't take their friend's rocks."

Fisher angled his head and gave Badger a pitying look. "Still surly about that? Oh Badger, let bygones be bygones."

"The Spider Eye Agate belonged to science," Badger hissed.

"Ho!" Fisher laughed. "Is 'the Spider Eye Agate' its scientific name then? And what did you know about science?" Fisher jabbed his walking stick at him. "Back then you were only a badger who'd found a pretty rock. If you could have seen yourself at the Weasel Family Reunion! Ho-ho!" He shook his head and chuckled. "All weekend long, there was Badger puttering around moon-eyed over an agate." He leaned in. "I probably did you a favor." Fisher put a paw in his trouser pocket and something jostled.

Badger couldn't help himself. He *had* to know. "What did you do with it?"

Fisher looked at him. "Ho! You still want *an agate*? An Important Rock Scientist like yourself? Ho-ho!" He drove his walking stick into the ground.

"You've got some nerve," Badger snarled.

Fisher nodded. "I do. I like to think I've got a lot of nerve." He removed his paw from his pocket, and held it out. "What do you think of these?"

Badger looked. It was a paw-full of tiny agates. One of the agates was stuck in basalt. Badger threw himself at it.

Fisher swiped his paw back. "Is that skunk your friend? Now that's unexpected! Badger with a skunk? You're about as welcoming as a sharp stick, and skunks?" Fisher lifted his luxurious tail and raised an eyebrow.

"Who I spend time with is none of your business." Badger crossed his arms and leaned.

"Ho-ho!" Fisher chuckled. "That skunk friend of yours was fast asleep under a tricornered hat with his rocks laid out in a little ring around him. How could I resist?" Fisher jostled the contents of his pocket.

"Get out of here, Fisher." Badger jerked his head in the direction of "out."

"Badger unwelcoming? Inhospitable? I never did understand what Aunt Lula saw in you. But family is family, and it must be tough making ends meet doing Important Rock Work of the agate variety." Fisher reached into his seersucker suit, pulled out a card, and waggled it in the air. "If you ever need help, this is how to get in touch."

Badger huffed.

Fisher set the card on a rock, looked at Badger, and then tapped the edge of his fedora with his walking stick. "You'll always be a weasel, Cousin." He turned, and Badger watched him make his way up the creek.

When Fisher was out of sight, Badger picked up the card. He read:

FISHER
TREASURE DEALER
I FIND WHAT CANNOT BE FOUND.
INQUIRIES TAKEN ON WEDNESDAYS
WESTERN WOODS, HOLLOW OAK WAY, SUITE 2302

"Abigshotnow," Aunt Lula had said of Fisher last time Badger had seen her. "Hedoesnotapproveofmyweaselfigurines."

Badger crossed the creek to find Skunk.

He found a skunk-shaped dent under the napping tree, but no Skunk.

Something red flip-flapped on the tree. Badger stepped closer. A piece of construction paper had been speared through with a twig. "BADGER" was written on the paper in a thick marker.

Badger freed the paper from its twig and read:

I have met a friend. I will meet you at Campsite #5 for dinner. —Skunk

P.S. I lost all my rocks in my sleep. Do rocks wander off? I know rocks roll, but now I am wondering about their wandering.

Did rocks wander? *Only with Fisher around!*

# CHAPTER SIX

*PFFFT. PFFFT. PFFFT.* BADGER HEARD THE SOUND AS HE approached Campsite #5.

Skunk's voice floated down the path. "But there is digging to do! Have you seen his digging claws? For him to be interested it would have to be very, very, *very* old."

*Must be that friend*, Badger thought.

When Skunk saw Badger coming up the path, he jumped up, bellows in paw. "Badger! There you are! Hello!" Badger sensed he was interrupting something.

Skunk gestured grandly at the sitting log. "We have a guest!"

The only thing Badger saw on the sitting log was Skunk's tricornered hat.

And then, Badger spotted her. Balanced on the third corner of the hat was a tiny orange hen the size of a pencil mug. Badger beamed. "Tiny Orange Hen!"

Skunk hissed, "Tiny Orange Hen is a description, not a name."

"She has a name?"

"Bock!" With a fluff, the hen gave Badger a look (first with her left eye, then her right eye, then her left. Blink, blink.) "Bock-bock-ga," said the hen pointedly.

Badger winced and cast Skunk a sidelong glance.

Skunk raised both eyebrows and nodded.

The tiny orange hen step-stepped toward Badger. "Bock-bock-ga." She looked at him right eye, left eye, up, down, blink. "Bock-bock-ga."

"Go on!" said Skunk.

"I can't!" said Badger.

"You can!"

"Sludge and slurry," Badger muttered. He took a deep breath and said it: "Bock. Bock. Ga?"

Skunk gasped. "Bock bock ga? She said 'Augusta'! She spoke so slowly too. Is it true that you *still* cannot understand the chicken dialect? 'Bock' is *not* a word."

Badger gave Skunk a look.

Skunk appraised Badger. "Yes. Regular lessons in the chicken dialect are necessary."

"Sorry," Badger mumbled. He spied a bag of chicken feed with a ladle in it. Next to the bag was the tricornered hat. The hat was filled with feed. Badger busied himself ladling more feed into the hat and then sat with his head in his paws.

There was a flutter and a scratch-scratch. He looked and saw her standing atop his knee.

*Tiny Orange Hen*! he thought. *No, Augusta. Say "Augusta."*

"Augusta," he managed to say.

"Bock," Augusta said, eyeing him (right, left, right).

Badger cleared his throat and said hesitantly, "I am so glad you're here, Augusta. You do know that you'd be welcome at the brownstone anytime?"

Augusta tilted her head. "Booock?" Her neck extended. She blink-blinked at him.

Badger nodded vigorously. "Absolutely. Anytime. I mean it. I'd always be delighted to see you."

"B-bock bock bock-bock?" Augusta stared at him (right eye, left eye, up-down).

Badger thought he understood. "Yes, you could visit me in my rock room. It would be an honor."

"Bock-bock." With a quick step-step, she hopped from his knee, then flap-fluttered to the tricornered hat and ate. All seemed well.

———◄◊►———

For dinner, Skunk cooked bread on flat (*basalt*) rocks. He also made wild garlic fried rice and a dandelion salad with an olive oil, mustard, and maple syrup vinaigrette. ("See all the dandelion greens? We have been sleeping in salad!") As he scooped up fried rice with his spork, Badger told Skunk and Augusta all about his cousin Fisher.

"That is a disturbing story," said Skunk. "A bad weasel (*a cousin!*) takes your Spider Eye Agate and gets away with it? Where is the comeuppance?"

"Fisher is at Endless Lake now."

Augusta's head shot out of her feathers. "Bock!"

Badger explained that Fisher was in the treasure trade. "There must be something he wants at Endless Lake. Still, he'll leave us alone. You cannot sell agates for enough money to interest a treasure trade dealer."

"Bock!" Augusta turned to Skunk. "Bock-bock-bocking. Bock-bock."

Skunk glanced at Badger and said not-quite-quietly enough, "But Augusta, I promised. I cannot just . . ." He looked at Badger and shut his mouth.

Badger frowned. "Promised what?"

Augusta and Skunk froze.

Badger looked between them and realized they did not want to tell him. This stung. He exhaled (*Fine!*) and decided to let it pass. "One other thing, Skunk. Fisher took your rocks. I saw your embedded agate in his paw, but I couldn't get it from him."

"So that is what happened!" Skunk waved a paw as if Badger's words were a cloud of gnats. "Do not worry about my agates, Badger. I will find more tomorrow. The finding is the best part! You should try panning for agates. I recommend it." Skunk paused for a moment, then grinned. "Hey, it is Sunday and I have not had one thought of the *New Yak Times Book Review*. I like rock-finding expeditions!"

Badger smiled.

The evening ended with stringing the backpacks into the tree. Then Skunk unrolled his sleeping bag in the middle of the clearing and put on his pajamas. "Goodnight," he said, and curled up to go to sleep.

Badger retired soon afterward. Inside his tent, he found Augusta roosting on his knapsack.

His ukulele lay in the far corner. Badger picked it up and plucked a string with a claw: *pling!*

Fisher was the last animal he wanted to run into.

He plucked another string: *pling!*

But agates were not treasure-trade quality—every animal knew this. Fisher was a busy weasel. He would leave them alone.

*Beed-el-lee-bing*, sounded the ukulele as he ran a claw over the strings.

"Bock-bick-beek-brrrring," Augusta sang.

Badger laughed. "Har! Goodnight, Augusta."

"Bock-bock." Augusta ruffled, then tucked her head under a wing.

Badger put down his ukulele, and crawled into his sleeping bag. *Tomorrow—agates. Important Rock Work. Focus . . . focus . . . fo . . .* And Badger fell asleep.

# CHAPTER SEVEN

"BRRRRRRRRRRRRRROCK. BRRROCK-BRRROCK-BRRROCK."

Badger opened his eyes and saw Augusta preening on top of his knapsack. "Morning Augusta," Badger said.

Augusta tilted her head and looked at him (right eye, left eye, blink-blink). "Bock." She fluttered off his knapsack, unzipped the tent, and left.

The door flip-flapped in the breeze. *Her name is Augusta.* Badger smiled and sat up. He pulled on his clothes. *Fire cocoa!*

——◄○►——

*Pfffft. Pfffft. Pfffft.* Skunk stoked the fire with his bellows. He wore the tricornered hat. Badger shuffled sleepily past him and pointed to the tree. "I'll get the backpacks."

Skunk set down the bellows and followed Badger. The talking began immediately. "I heard you last night. You were out looking for a snack. Badger, I brought plenty of food! There have not been as many picnics as I expected, and so far, Augusta is our only guest."

*I was not out here last night.* Badger shuffled drowsily forward. *Fire cocoa. Need fire cocoa.*

Skunk kept up. "There is no use denying it, Badger. I heard you! Plod. Plod. Snuffle. Like that! Also, your breath was a punch to the snout! All I am saying is that you do not have to put the backpacks into the tree anymore. Keep the backpacks on the ground and have your midnight snacks. Have snacks with bears! Or whoever else wants one!"

*Plod? Do I plod?* Badger put a claw into the knot and worked it loose. He had a vague feeling he had heard plodding in the middle of the night. And what had Skunk said about his breath? Badger recalled it, clamped his mouth shut, and glanced at Skunk as he unwound the rope.

Skunk slapped his paw against the tree trunk and leaned. "What do you say, Badger? How about some sharing?"

Badger stopped his pulleying. "One does not share with bears. Also, I was not out last night looking for a snack."

Skunk huffed. "Breathe on me!"

Badger could see he wasn't going to get his fire cocoa until he did it. "Huuuuuuh," he breathed.

"Hoo!" Skunk waved a paw and stepped back. "However, your breath was worse last night."

"Not my breath!" Badger said. "*And* I do not plod. I pad! There is a difference."

"Yes, an *A* and an *L*. Also, an *O*."

"Skunk, only *big* animals plod."

"How big?" Skunk looked him over. "You are plenty big for several plods and a snuffle."

Badger gazed up into the tree. "*Bear* big."

Skunk looked wide-eyed into the woods. "Perhaps we should continue hanging the backpacks in the tree."

———◄◦►———

They hauled the yellow backpack to the firepit, and Badger hurried off to do some breath maintenance. While brushing his teeth, Badger heard: "I promised Badger. Are you sure this is necessary?"

"BOCK. Bock-bock!"

"What is necessary?" Badger asked upon joining them.

At his question, Skunk and Augusta went silent. Skunk held a ladle full of batter. Augusta stood on the tricornered hat. They blinked up at him. And said nothing!

Badger stared. What was going on? He could really use some fire cocoa!

"Ah, Badger?" Skunk set down the ladle, moved the frying pan off the fire, and met Badger's gaze with a definite cringe. "Would you mind if I went off with Augusta today? She has something she wants to show me. Tomorrow, I promise to look for agates with you."

*Something is up*, Badger thought as he chugged fire cocoa. He lowered the mug and managed, "Sure. It's only one day." As he ate his breakfast of johnnycakes and jam, Badger decided to follow them.

———◄○►———

Badger cleaned the dishes quickly. He pulleyed the backpacks up into the tree. He threaded his arms through his knapsack straps and spoke loudly and clearly: "Important Rock Work. Focus. Focus. Focus." As he started down the path to Endless Lake, he called out, "Have a good day! Off I go!" When he was out of sight, Badger doubled back and tucked himself behind a tree with a view of Campsite #5.

Badger did not need to wait behind the tree for long. Skunk threw on his knapsack and put on his tricornered hat. Augusta adjusted a chicken-sized headlamp on her head and then, with a hop-hop-flutter, landed on Skunk's hat. She settled herself behind the front point and waved a wing in the direction of the woods. "Bock!"

With a skip and a leap, Skunk set off.

Badger followed. Behind trees, he zigged. Around boulders, he zagged. Badger ducked down and popped up with precision. He looked before he leapt. He crept. He tip-clawed, tip-clawed, and dove behind logs. He slithered for sightings. He looked all ways . . . and? *Go!* He raced to the next tree and stood up. He pressed his back against tree trunks and scooted. (*Stealthy!*) He spied Skunk folding over and slapping his knees. "Ha ha ha ha ha!" The hat tilted. Augusta clung by a foot. "BOCK! B-bock!" Skunk shot upright. "Forgot–no bending, no bowing, no sweeping my hat off to say 'how do.'" Augusta circled a wing. "Bock!" And again, they were off.

Badger trailed Augusta and Skunk through woods, up and down hills. Now they traversed a ridge. Now they came to a meadow. At the end of the meadow was a huge rock face.

*Nowhere to hide!* Badger looked in both directions, squinted at the rock face (*gabbro intrusion*), and dropped into the grass. He landed (*ow!*) on a porphyritic rhyolite rock. An urge to examine the rock came over him.

*Do not touch the rhyolite!*

Badger touched the rhyolite.

His mind plunged into the deep place. With a claw, he scraped at a pink feldspar crystal, then the white quartz. *The crystals are conspicuous.* He scratched at the red rhyolite. *Igneous.* In his mind, lava erupted. Badger blinked back to the rock. *A typical example of porphyritic rhyolite.* He tossed the rock aside and saw where he was.

He was standing in the meadow. *In plain sight!*

It should have been disaster.

But Badger was alone. He faced a huge gabbro rock face. Where were Skunk and Augusta? They were not *upon* the gabbro rock face. Or *beside* it. Not this way. Or that way. "Not possible . . . not possible," Badger muttered as he turned in a complete circle.

It was a dead end, and he had lost Skunk and Augusta.

# CHAPTER EIGHT

BADGER POUNDED HIS PAW ON THE GABBRO ROCK FACE. Then he sighed heavily, rested his forehead against the rock, and closed his eyes.

A faint sound: "Bock-bock."

"Who is there?"

Quickly, Badger pressed his ear to the rock and heard: "Bock-bock bock-bock." "Orange snout, green snout who?" Followed by: "Ha! Good one!" and "See how I did not lean over this time?"

*Skunk!* Badger looked both ways, then up and down. *There has to be a way in. Or around. Or under. Where? Where?* He paced the length of the rock face. *A broken twig! And an orange feathery tuft!* Badger pinched the tuft up. *Hm.* He pushed aside the twig and saw a chicken-sized path. He followed it. The path wandered. It looped twice, made one bend, and ended at a hole.

Badger picked up a pebble. Remembering the rhyolite, he dropped the pebble into the hole unexamined.

The pebble hit the bottom with a high "chip!"

The "chip!" echoed: *CHIP-CHip-chi*.

"Ah!" Badger said. He flourished his digging claws and dug the hole out. Then he dropped into it.

He landed ("UNg.") on a rock surface in the dark.

*UNg-Ung-ung*, sounded the echo.

A puff of cool, damp air.

*A cave!*

It took a moment for Badger's eyes to adjust, and then he saw he stood in a large cavern. A light flick-flick-flicked from a passage on the far side. *Augusta's headlamp!* His heartbeat quickened. Badger followed the light across the cavern and into the passageway. Skunk's voice came loud and clear: "It is not an easy job, Augusta. We need help."

The light took on a warm yellow glow, as if Augusta's headlamp had illuminated something golden. *Gold? At Endless Lake?* Gold made no geological sense. Badger tried to dislodge the idea. But what else could it be?

*A cave!*

He wanted to know. Badger loped down the passageway, slipped into the back of the chamber, and felt his jaw fall.

Before him? A wall made of amber. *Amber. Gold-colored.* And that wasn't all! In the middle of the amber wall was an egg—a fossilized egg. It was an egg of unlikely size. The egg was three times as big as Badger. *At least!*

The enormous fossilized egg hung in a wall of amber.

Skunk and Augusta had not noticed him. They stood farther in, closer to the wall, their backs to him, engaged in a heated discussion. But Badger no longer cared if they saw him. *The egg! The egg!* He'd never seen such an egg!

And there was something more too. He was sure he had seen something *in* the egg, glimpsed something. Or he thought he had. It hardly seemed possible. *Light! Need more light!* Badger slipped off his knapsack, unzipped it, and rummaged. Finally, Badger's paw closed over the cool metal barrel of the X34 Mighty Blaze, the flashlight preferred by badger rock scientists everywhere. "A star in your pocket!" the advertisements boasted. Badger did not know about *that*, but the Mighty Blaze certainly packed enough lumens to light up a room.

Or—in this case—an egg. Badger pointed and *c-click*-ed the rubber button.

Light flooded.

Badger groaned. "EGG! MARKS! THE SPOT!"

Light from a chicken-sized headlamp flicked into his eyes. Badger heard: "It is too late, Augusta. He has seen it."

"Bockety-bock!"

"Yes, Badger has behaved badly."

"Bock!"

"He snuck."

"Bock bockle."

"He spied."

"Bockety bockety bock!"

"But Augusta, Badger is here now, and badgers are well known for their excavation skills. Look at those digging claws. We could put those to good use." There was a hiss in Badger's ear: "I was trying to convince her to ask for your help!"

But Badger barely heard this. He held his X34 Mighty Blaze flashlight steady. He aimed the flashlight at the egg. The light beamed out and *through*—through the amber, through the eggshell, *and* . . .

"Oh," Badger gasped, his heart melting. Inside the egg a dinosaur curled. Its heavily lidded eyes were closed as if it were only asleep. ("Shhhhh!" Badger nearly said.)

Augusta murmured a low "b-bock-bock-bock."

"Is it sucking its tail?" Skunk asked.

Yes! The dinosaur appeared to be sucking its tail!

X34 Mighty Blaze in paw, Badger stumbled toward the amber egg with dinosaur. "What an egg! Cretaceous or Jurassic? . . . Jurassic . . . Yes, Jurassic. Why didn't you tell me? Why didn't you come to me first?" Badger held his paw up as if caught. "I know, I know. I usually don't have time for dinosaurs. But this? THIS EGG? The sublimity. The texture. The way it shimmers. And with a dinosaur inside?" Badger shook his head in wonder. "Science and art! Beauty and power! FRAGILITY AND STRENGTH. Science will flourish! Knowledge will prosper! Oh, the discoveries that will result from such inspiration!"

Badger could scarcely draw breath. He strode back and forth, Mighty Blaze in paw. His life's purpose shimmered in amber before him. The egg–the dinosaur!–was the reason he lived and breathed and dug. He *must* lay hold. He *must* step forward and grasp. Curation! He *must* collect, install, and light.

Badger took a step toward the egg.

Augusta broke into a wild, flip-flapping ruckus. "BOCK! Bock-bock-bocket." Something hammered Badger hard in the shin. Pain! But Badger's eyes remained fixed on the amber egg.

Skunk clutched his arm. "BADGER, stop. STOP. Please? Augusta told me you would do this. She said you would become eggnotized. EGG-NO-TIZED. Resist, Badger, RESIST."

Badger shook Skunk off.

"This is not for science, Badger. This is for chickens. The chickens have been watching this egg for a long, long time."

"Brrr-bock-bockle."

Badger heard her. "Chickens?" he said. He looked away from the egg and saw Augusta. Augusta jerked her head (right, left, right). She swung one wing, then the other. "Bock! Bockle!" She marched. "Bockety! Bock-bock-bockle!"

Badger suddenly understood. He looked at Skunk. "How long have the chickens been watching this egg?"

"For generations! Hens of hens of hens of hens (and probably many more hens). We must move the egg. Use your digging claws for good, Badger!" Skunk nodded. "You are not the only danger. Word has gotten out."

"Bock!"

"Word is out? Who?"

"Only little old me," said a voice behind them.

# CHAPTER NINE

*THAT* VOICE—BADGER FROZE.

"Isn't that dinosaur adorable? Ho-ho! Egg marks the spot indeed!"

"Fisher," Badger hissed. He turned. Skunk and Augusta turned with him.

"Cousin!" Fisher said, shielding his eyes from the spot of light beaming from Augusta's headlamp. "What happened to your Important Rock Work? Wasn't it agates? Where's that focus, focus, focus?"

Badger clenched a paw and swallowed hard. Then he gave Augusta a nod and stepped forward. "Fisher, listen. This isn't a treasure to—"

"Treasure? What would you know about treasure?" Fisher interrupted. "Anyway, dinosaurs, fossils, eggs in amber are hardly your thing. Remember what you told me at the Weasel Family Reunion?"

"Fisher, the egg isn't to be taken and sold," Badger said with urgency.

"Now why can't I remember your exact words?" Fisher's eyes drifted into the dark depths above them.

"Fisher—the egg! It's personal. It has significant meaning for an entire group of animals. They've been caring for this egg for a long, long time. You must leave the egg here!"

"Bock! Bock-bockle bock bock!"

Fisher snapped his claws and pointed at Badger. "Got it! You said dinosaurs, all that fossil-ly stuff, was too juvenile, too adolescent, *not old enough* to be of interest. You said you only studied rocks *before* dinosaurs. I recall a sneer. I did think it snooty of you. But no matter, plenty of clients adore this stuff. They are—I grant you—romantics every one." He looked at the egg and moaned. "Aw, a baby dinosaur? Irresistible. Ho-ho! Have you ever seen such a beauty? Badger, I am happy to take your castoffs. You can have the agates, the lava, and the Precambrian slime."

Badger huffed. "Precambrian stromatolites are living rocks, rocks made up of cyanobacteria that secrete lime. They are not slime. Show some respect."

Beside him, Skunk said to Augusta, "Why does he only talk to Badger? We are here too. Are we invisible? I do not think so!"

"Bock!"

Badger saw Skunk's tail flip off the floor and hissed, "Skunk, let me take care of this."

Badger faced Fisher and dropped to his knees. "I beg you, Fisher. Leave the egg." He raised his clenched paws and shook them. "Please, Fisher, please."

Shocked silence followed.

Then: "Ho-ho-ho-ho! Ho-ho-ho!" Fisher wiped his eyes with a silk hankie, then pocketed it. "On your knees? Pretty please, Fisher? Ho! If Aunt Lula . . . Ho-ho! . . . could see you now! Ho!"

Badger got up off his knees.

"Enough chitchat." Fisher met Badger's gaze with eyes sharp as tacks. "Badger, it's time for you and your little friends to skedaddle. The professionals have work to do. Now that passage there," Fisher gestured at the passageway where they'd arrived, ". . . leads in and out. If the three of you leave now, I'll let you use it. Otherwise, I cannot be responsible if you *accidentally* get in the way." Fisher settled both paws on his walking stick and raised an eyebrow.

Skunk stepped forward. "We are not going anywhere. You are not taking that egg."

Augusta fluttered onto Skunk's shoulder, headlamp blazing. "BOCK." (Right eye.) "BOCK." (Left eye.) "BOCK." (Up-down.) A spot of light crossed Fisher's face one way, then the other way, then furry chin to fedora.

Fisher blinked with irritation. "Fine. Stay if you must."

He turned toward the passageway. "IN HERE," he bellowed.

From the passage came the sound of scrabbling.

"LET'S GO. LET'S GO. LET'S GO," called Fisher.

The scrabbling grew louder.

Augusta's headlamp flicked into the dark passage. Eye upon eye upon eye glowed back–hundreds of glowing red eyes.

"Eyeshine. Red. Rat," whispered Skunk.

A tumbling surge of rats rushed in. The rats wore hard hats.

With a flap-flap-flutter, Augusta landed on Skunk's hat and switched her headlamp off.

"FIND THE ROCK EDGES," Fisher barked. "LEAVE THE AMBER. DO NOT TOUCH THE EGG."

Badger and Skunk (with Augusta now anchored in a curl of tricornered hat) speedily backed up. Badger spied a high, level spot at one side of the chamber. He pointed. "Up! Onto that ledge!"

Skunk and Badger dashed for the slide of rocks beneath the ledge. Hot, ratty breath pressed upon their backs. As their feet left the cave floor, a sweep of rats covered it.

The ledge was higher than it had looked from below, and the rock looser. Each step sent rock (*shale-y limestone*) showering down. They reached the ledge and doubled over, out of breath.

Badger gulped for air and scanned the area. The ledge was level with the egg. Between the ledge and the egg there was . . . Badger stepped forward to investigate. *A considerable gap!* And the only way out appeared to be the way they had come in.

Now rats in brightly colored hard hats poured through the passageway. They channeled around Fisher to get at the wall that held the amber egg. First came rats wearing reflective harnesses jingling with carabiners. They carried rope, hammers, pitons, and anchors. The hammers drove anchors into rock and pitons into cracks. *Kling-kling-kling!* The rope was looped and hitched and pulled (*sh-sh-sh*). Carabiners were *k-clip*ped. Next came the free-climbing rats who scrambled on top of the harnessed rats, using the harnessed rats as pawholds and footholds. The cavern grew loud with their sounds: *Kling-kling-kling! K-clip. K-clip. Sh-sh-sh.* Behind Fisher, a small team of rats worked to organize equipment (rope, net, extra hard hats) and rat comforts (drinks, snacks, and rat-sized tubs of paw and claw cream).

"We are stuck on this ledge," Badger said to Skunk and Augusta.

Skunk leaned forward for a look. "Yes. This does not look promising."

Augusta strode back and forth. She stopped now and again to peer and look (right, left, right). "Brrroooock bock," she said in a low voice.

Fisher stood in the center of the cavern floor, rocking in his lemon-yellow loafers, tap-tap-tapping his walking stick. A smile played on his lips. The rats were everywhere. Badger squinted at one. "They're wharf rats." Wharf rats were the big ones. Some of these rats were nearly as big as Skunk.

Augusta nodded (up, down, up). "BOCK-bockle."

Skunk frowned at both of them. "Egg-suckers? Wharf rats? No! Those rats like to be called Norway rats." He leaned forward to whisper. "There are rumors that these particular rats are descended from rats that came across the ocean in boxes of grain on Hessian warships in 1776. Can you imagine? You travel all that way eating only groats, barley, and flour, and then: *Bam!* The ship runs aground. 'Land ho!' *Finally!* you think as you run out of your barley box and dodge the whacking sticks and stomping boots. (If you are a rat, sticks and boots is the expected greeting.) But you have landed! You are thinking, *I am here! Land of plenty! Ground under my paws!* Unfortunately it is 1776 and you are in the middle of a war."

Badger saw the egg was surrounded by rats in hard hats. Rat brown and safety orange covered the golden amber wall. He heard a whistle, a hoot, then a holler. Several rat heads popped up and looked around. A tail flicked and pointed. Across the way, a tail bent and swooshed. Several tails went upright, and Badger heard high-pitched laughter. Then: "Rope!" And: "Piton!" Also: "Clip!" Something metal was pounded into rock: *Kling-kling-kling!*

Skunk continued, "Landing in the middle of a war after a long journey explains a lot about Norway rats: self-determination, rugged individualism, and all that 'rats are the best—rah, rah, rah!'" Skunk looked at the amber egg and winced. "If you want a job done, a team of Norway rats is the way to go. Good climbers. Chisel-chewers too. Norway rats will have the egg off the wall in no time."

There was a new sound: *Skra-ska. Skra-ska. Skra. Sk-sk-sk.* A rat raised its head, wiped its mouth. *Chisel-chewing.* The rats were chewing the amber and the egg right out of the rock. Badger blinked at Skunk. "How do you know so much about rats?"

Skunk did not answer him. Instead, he pointed. "Look, a spotlight!"

Indeed! A long line of rats with a spotlight on a pole resting on their shoulders emerged from the passageway. A second spotlight followed. The rats kicked open stands. They adjusted the height. They aimed the spotlights at the amber egg.

Augusta's head flicked between each spotlight and the egg.

Skunk said, "We have to do something. We need an idea. Think, think, think."

*Skra-ska. SK.*

The first spotlight turned on. *Bhoof!*

The second spotlight turned on. *Bhoof!*

Light flooded the chamber. The shadows fled. The amber egg lit up like a meteor. The chisel-chewing stopped.

There it was: the dinosaur! The dinosaur curled inside the egg.

All up and down the wall, rat heads popped up and twisted.

"Look at all those colors!" Skunk gushed. "I thought dinosaurs only came in one dingy green color."

Augusta stretched out her neck. "B-booock?"

*Pigment? On a dinosaur?* But yes, the spotlights had illuminated colors! The dinosaur was a mottled olive with shades of eggplant. Its eyelids were lavender-blue. There was a yellow horn.

A chattering commenced. Tails bent, waved, and pointed. Some tails spiraled, others swooshed. Then the rats broke out in whistles and hoots and "Oooooooohs."

Badger gazed at the little dinosaur and a lump rose in his throat. *So unaware of the amber tree sap that lay in its future.*

Lumps in his throat? Was he an Important Rock Scientist or not? *Detach! Use the dispassionate eye!* Badger inhaled and gave himself a stern talking-to: *It is an embryonic dinosaur. A near hatchling.* And above all else, this near hatchling was a fossil—a trace, a hint, a preservation of its former embryonic self.

But Badger looked again, and all was lost. His heart pounded with fondness for the little dinosaur asleep in the amber egg. With a start, Badger realized the last time he had felt so engaged had been all those years ago when he'd gazed into his Spider Eye Agate.

Fisher put his paws to his mouth. "JAWS TO THE GRINDSTONE! YES, YES WE'VE GOT AN ADORABLE TREASURE ON OUR PAWS. LET'S TAKE CARE. NO DODGY CLIPS AND NO FRAYED ROPE."

One rat whistled. Another whistled in reply. A flip of a tail. A head jerked. Hoots. Hollering. *Kling-kling-kling! Skra-ska. Sk-sk-sk.*

Badger squinted into the far corners of the chamber, hoping to see something, anything, that might spark an idea.

*Skra-ska. Skra-ska.*

A loud *CRACK!*

All three of them raced to the edge.

"CAREFUL NOW," Fisher called.

Badger braced himself and leaned to look. A length of the wall had been chewed through.

A pop! *Sk-sk-sk.* There was a low crackling. A runnel of pebbles hit the floor. The rats broke into chatter. A tail swirled, then jab-jab-jabbed. Rats whistled here, over there. "Steady! Steady . . . steady," said a rat in a hard hat and harness.

"CHECK THE ANCHORS. PITON ON THE LEFT!"

*Skra-ska. Sk-sk-sk.*

The amber was beginning to move freely.

"We need an idea and we need it now," said Skunk.

Badger glanced at Augusta and suddenly an idea came. "What about the Quantum Leap? Couldn't the chickens do something with the Quantum Leap?"

Skunk blinked. "Of course! The chicken whistle!"

"Chicken whistle?" Badger gasped. "I said 'the Quantum Leap!'"

But Skunk wasn't listening to him. "What do you think, Augusta?"

A mysterious look passed over Augusta's face. She settled her feet and rolled her toes on the rock. She considered the egg (left eye, right eye, left eye). Then she turned to the two of them with her eyelids half shut. "BOCK," she said with a serious nod.

Skunk pulled the whistle from his pocket.

Badger grimaced, remembering the last time the chicken whistle had been blown, and braced himself. *I am a badger, not a chicken. As a badger, I cannot hear a whistle meant for chickens. Therefore, I will not hear the chicken whistle.*

Skunk blew the chicken whistle and the most awful sound assailed Badger's ears. It was as if an entire herd of mosquito-sized elephants trumpeted inside his head.

*I AM NOT A CHICKEN*, Badger thought as he crumpled onto the ledge.

*Pad, pad, pad.* Hind feet approaching. "What are you doing down there?" Skunk's face came in close. "Have you responded this poorly to stress in the past? Breathe in through your snout and out through your mouth."

"Go away."

Skunk waved the chicken whistle in Badger's face. "Do not worry, reinforcements are on the way. Chickens are coming!"

He nodded and looked around the cavern expectantly. "It is so convenient to have a whistle that *only* chickens can hear."

Badger got up and saw that Fisher and the rats worked as if nothing had happened and groaned. "Badgers are not chickens," he muttered through clenched teeth.

*Skra-sk-sk-sk. Kling-kling-kling*! The rats in hard hats were stabilizing the egg and amber in order to lower the entire piece to the cavern floor.

Augusta now stood halfway up a big rock. She studied the egg with a faraway look in her left eye, right eye, left eye. "Brrrrock," she murmured with a blink and a tilt. "Brrrock bock."

Badger followed her gaze to the dinosaur curled in its egg. That was when Badger saw it—the flick, flick, flick of the dinosaur's tail.

# CHAPTER TEN

FLICK, FLICK, FLICK.

Badger stared. He rubbed his eyes and looked again.

*Yes!* The dinosaur's tail appeared to be flicking. *I am losing my mind.* Badger clamped his eyes closed. *Focus, focus, focus,* he told himself. *Be an Important Rock Scientist.* He opened one—then two—dispassionate eyes.

And saw a whole new side to the dinosaur! Badger set one paw on a rock to steady himself, and gestured frantically with the other. "Skunk, SKUNK! Was the . . . ? Before . . . ? Do you remember . . . ?"

Skunk, who had been turned in hopes of spotting chicken reinforcements, twisted around and gaped. "Wasn't the dinosaur sucking its tail? Where *is* the dinosaur's tail?" He blinked hard.

The dinosaur somersaulted.

"AHHHHHH!" screamed Badger and Skunk together.

The dinosaur jolted upright and *ram, ram, rammed* the shell. Skunk hopped up and down and pointed. "Egg tooth! Egg tooth! Egg tooth!"

*EGG TOOTH . . . EGG tooth . . . egg tooth,* came an echo.

The cavern had gone quiet. Where was the chisel-chewing? Where were the bright *kling-kling-kling*s*?*

The rats in hard hats had stopped. They watched the egg. Snouts twitched in the air. Whiskers vibrated. Heads tilted. A tail jabbed up, up, up. Badger glanced at the cavern floor and saw Fisher leaning on his walking stick as if he actually required it. Then Badger scanned the cavern—the farthest reaches, the darkest corners. *Where are the chickens?*

Badger looked back at the amber egg and saw a ribbon of spine, the backs of two hind feet. The rib cage moved (in-out, in-out).

Badger looked at Skunk and then at Augusta, who stood off by herself, halfway up the big rock, with *that look* in her eyes (left, right, left, blink-blink). Badger gestured at the egg. "This is *not* possible. *This* is an unhatched egg covered in amber, an egg fossilized hundreds of millions of years ago. A glop of tree sap lands on the egg. The sappy egg is covered by silt from a stream. (Or perhaps a flood.) Here's the thing: an eggshell is a membrane that lets air *in* and lets air *out*. Eggshells breathe! But this eggshell was covered by sap, then silt—muck upon muck. No air—no breath! Life was not sustained! Therefore: the dinosaur is not alive."

Skunk gave him a confused look. "The baby dinosaur has moved *several* times. Remember how the baby dinosaur used to be sucking its tail? It is not sucking its tail now."

Badger ignored this and continued: "So why hatch today? Why wait hundreds of millions of years for today? What is so special about today?"

Skunk shrugged. "Does anyone choose their birthday?"

Badger groaned and wished for a more scientifically inclined roommate. He recalled that chickens understood physics and cast a hopeful glance at Augusta. Augusta was not paying attention. She was climbing her rock—one flutter, one hop at a time. She stopped, gave Badger a strange day-dreamy look (right-left-right), then turned and climbed higher.

Unexpectedly, two words popped into Badger's head: "modern birds." It was something from his paleontology class, Dino 101.

There was something he needed to recall. Badger watched Augusta climb higher and remembered his professor writing on the blackboard. *Yes!* His professor had been sketching out a family tree. In his mind, Badger heard his professor's voice (a voice that carried in the way only a cockatoo's voice could carry) say, "Modern birds descended from dinosaurs."

*Chickens! Chickens are modern birds.*

Badger turned to Skunk. "Modern birds descended from dinosaurs. You blew the chicken whistle!"

Skunk frowned at Badger. "Badger, only *chickens* hear the chicken whistle."

(At this juncture, it did occur to Badger to tell Skunk that this wasn't strictly true, but was this the time?)

Badger looked at Skunk and said slowly, "Chickens *are* modern birds."

Skunk went slack-jawed. "Dinosaurs are chickens?" His head swiveled to stare at Augusta.

"*Or* chickens are dinosaurs," Badger muttered, as he also stared at Augusta.

Augusta was now at the top of her rock. The rock stood on the edge of the drop. Across the drop was the wall that held the egg.

"What is she doing?" said Badger as he watched her cling to the side of her rock and stretch-stretch-stretch in the direction of the egg.

"Augusta!" Skunk called.

Augusta paid them no attention. She leaned out, out, out and into the light from Fisher's spotlights. Her orange feathers blazed. Badger was reminded of a tiny lantern set upon a rocky crag.

Then she began to make a sound—a long, low burbling sound.

"Is that a song?" Badger asked. The sound reminded Badger less of singing and more of a brook running over round stones, the water steadily, steadily filling every space, rolling over the old and dry and left behind.

"I think it is a lullaby," said Skunk. There was a pause as Skunk thought. Then he looked at Badger. "I know it was my idea to blow the chicken whistle. But Augusta endorsed the idea—strongly, I might add. I thought I was calling for chicken reinforcements. I thought that is what she thought too, but now I am not sure. Did she know the chicken whistle would wake the dinosaur?"

*CRRRrraaaAAAACK!*

A bright yellow horn smashed through eggshell, then amber. Fluid gushed. A splatter! Eggshell, amber, and rock hit the cavern floor and splintered.

Out burst a dinosaur head! The dinosaur wore an eggshell cap. Its lavender-blue eyelid blinked open. A golden eye. The

*Outside the shell,*

*the dinosaur seemed bigger.*

dinosaur let out a piercing "ArrrRRRRRRRUUK!" Then the dinosaur turned to Augusta. "Aar-ROOP? Roop-roop?"

"Bock," said Augusta, suddenly clear-eyed (blink-blink). She focused on the dinosaur and continued her burbling lullaby.

Skunk and Badger exchanged incredulous looks.

The dinosaur tossed the shell off its head—*Feathers! Twiggy feathers!*—and then the dinosaur rocked against the side of the egg. *Ram! Ram! Ram!* Rock screeched and dropped to the cavern floor. The dinosaur kicked off the last shard of shell and stepped free.

Badger gawked as the dinosaur shook out its hind legs and stood upright on them. A lengthy, feathered tail was unfurled, a feathered collar straightened and stretched and fluffed. Outside the shell, the dinosaur seemed bigger. It wasn't three times Badger's size—more like four times. Also, one toe on each hind foot was raised off the ground. The nails on the upturned toes looked unusually sharp.

"Aaar-roop? Roop?" The dinosaur stretched its neck in Augusta's direction. It tilted its head one way (right eye), then the other (left eye) to look at her. Its tail whipped back and forth.

Fisher's voice rose from the floor of the cavern: "WE TAKE THE DINOSAUR ALIVE!"

The rats in hard hats stirred as one. There was a hoot. A whistle came from the far end. *Kling-kling-kling! K-clip! K-clip! Sh-sh-sh.*

Rope in paw, the first rat crept toward the dinosaur.

And then, in a movement so fast Badger wasn't sure he saw it, the dinosaur pinned the rope with the toenail on its upturned toe and slurped up the rat.

# CHAPTER ELEVEN

"SLURPED UP A RAT!" SKUNK YELLED IN HORROR.

The dinosaur tossed back its head and swallowed hard. Its eyes grew wide. It blinked several times. There was a pause, and then—

"AaRRAUK! RAUK!" The dinosaur stomp-stomp-stomped.

As one who often felt like beating his chest after a meal made by Skunk, Badger understood. Rat tasted good.

"Oh no-no-no! I did not want to see that." Skunk waved his paws in front of his face.

Pandemonium broke out. It was every rat for themselves. Rats rappelled off the wall. They jumped. Waves of rats scrambled over the backs of their chisel-chewing colleagues on their way to the chamber floor.

Skunk was at the edge waving his tricornered hat. "Get off the wall! Not a vegetarian! Quicker than you think!"

Over the havoc came Fisher's voice: "IT'S A BIG BABY! ARE RATS AFRAID OF BABIES?"

Badger scanned for Augusta and found her on top of her rock, silently watching the rats in hard hats (that, over there, across the way). She flicked her head back to the dinosaur (right eye, left eye, up, up . . . up-down).

The dinosaur speared a climbing rope with the toenail on its upturned toe. "Rauk-rauk."

*Toenail?* Badger squinted. *That is a claw!*

Augusta leaned out and began singing her burbling lullaby again. That was when a voice behind him said, "Would you look at you!"

Badger turned and saw a rat in a hard hat—a grimy one with a huge yellow-toothed grin smeared across its face. The rat carried a clipboard.

"What do you want?" Badger growled.

"SCRATCH!"

*Skunk?* Badger turned and saw Skunk hop into the air, then race for the rat. After a hug, Skunk and the rat pounded each other on the back.

The rat jabbed a dirt-encrusted claw at Skunk's hat. "I saw that tricorner and I thought, 'Only one skunk would wear a tricornered hat!'"

Beaming, Skunk took Scratch by the elbow and led the rat over. "Badger, Scratch. Scratch, Badger. Scratch was my neighbor when I lived under the bridge beneath the, ah, second blue dumpster. She is the *best* neighbor and also, the best food delivery service. So gourmet! Maple syrup, fermented lemons, and pawpaws—in season, of course. Have you had a pawpaw? Pawpaws taste like banana cream pie *with no baking*, which is helpful for quick and easy dessert courses when you cook on a number-ten tin-can stove."

Badger blinked. "You lived *beneath* a dumpster?"

Skunk ignored him and smiled broadly at Scratch.

Scratch slugged Skunk in the arm. "I miss your hobo stew, kid. Still have that red suitcase?"

"Ha! Your twine keeps it shut!" Skunk pointed. "That is a fine clipboard. You always did have exceptional organizational capabilities. Is this your team of rats?" Grinning, Skunk turned to the wall. His face fell. "Oh."

The wall was rapidly emptying of rats in hard hats. They left behind a litter of muddled rope, carabiners, and rock riddled with pitons and anchors.

Scratch chucked her chin at the wall. "Rat Guild 73–what's left of us."

Skunk gave Scratch a serious look. "You have to get out of here. It is not safe for rats."

"What a catastrophe! A real tragedy!" Scratch took off her hard hat, scrubbed her head with the inside of her arm, and then screwed the hat back on. "Rat guild rats are used to putting their lives on the line, but not from treasure-come-to-life! Remove amber with fossilized egg? Sure, we'll sign on that dotted line. But you show me where in the rat guild rulebook it says we're obligated to plate ourselves as spaghetti."

Augusta's burbling lullaby filled the pause that followed.

Scratch cast a concerned glance at Augusta. "You gotta turn that chicken off. She is snack-sized."

Badger looked at Augusta, then at the dinosaur. Happily, the dinosaur was preoccupied with the climbing ropes dangling from its toes. It shook one foot, then the other. "Rrauk! Rrauk!" The ropes rattled and snapped in the air.

On the cavern floor, rats in hard hats hastily gathered up personal belongings along with extra supplies (rope, netting, tarps, bungee cords, safety vests, hard hats, harnesses, climbing odds and ends, and all toolboxes).

Skunk and Scratch joined Badger and the three of them watched Fisher talk to one passing rat, then the next. Badger heard the words "double pay," "overtime," "fame, honor, glory." It did no good. Rat after rat pressed onward, stopping only at the cooler for juice boxes and paw-fulls of string cheese.

Scratch groaned. "That weasel has some nerve. ROSHA is going to hear about this!"

Skunk whispered: "ROSHA—Rat Occupational Safety and Health Administration."

"AAAaaaaRAUk!"

At the sound, all three froze. Badger saw the dinosaur's ropes had tangled (*Ss-CLUNK. Ss-CLUNK*) . . . and untangled (*ss-snap-snap*).

This was followed by Augusta's burbled singing.

"Enough of this," Scratch muttered. She clamped the clipboard under her elbow, put two claws in her mouth, and whistled. Her tail shot up, then circled. "We're outta here. Nice to see you, kid."

Again, Skunk and Scratch pounded each other on the back.

Scratch gave Badger a terse nod, then fixed Skunk with a stern look. "You three need to get outta here. Grab the chicken and go."

"Yes, I will convince her." Skunk trotted the dozen feet to the base of her rock and called out, "Augusta? It is time to go!"

This was when—*Bhoof!*—the first spotlight went out.

"AaaRAUK!" The dinosaur stomped. A rope fell from a toe. Pebbles rained down.

Skunk said, "Did you hear what I said? It is time to leave."

"BADGER? COUSIN?" Fisher's voice filled the cavern.

Badger stepped forward. He glimpsed Scratch and a second rat disappearing into the passageway with the cooler.

Fisher continued, "TAKE CARE OF MY DINOSAUR. I'LL BE BACK TO COLLECT IT."

"SORRY, FISHER. WE'RE NOT STICKING AROUND."

"THAT'S WHAT YOU THINK. Ho-ho!" Fisher reached with his walking stick.

*Bhoof!*—the second light went out, and everything went dark.

"RaUUUK!"

"Sludge and slurry."

A light beamed out. Badger twisted around and saw Augusta had turned on her headlamp. The beam shone steadily across the gap onto the top of the wall, where the dinosaur now stood.

Skunk said, "What won't I like, Augusta? What do you mean, I will not like it but you are going to do it anyway? What do you mean, it is for the best? Augusta, please come down now."

But Augusta wasn't listening. Augusta leaned toward the dinosaur and sang.

"Roop? Roop?" The dinosaur called.

In the cavern below, Badger heard footsteps: *T-tap, tap. T-tap, tap.* Fisher, walking with his stick in lemon-yellow loafers. The footsteps grew distant. *T-tap, tap.*

Badger's eyes adjusted. He could see now the chamber below was empty.

*T-tap, tap.* The sound came from inside the passageway. *T-tap.* The footsteps stopped. There was a riffle through pockets. Something rattled in a box. A quiet *snap-snap-SCRITCH.* "There it goes. Ho-ho!"

Badger heard *ssss...*"GOOD LUCK, COUSIN!" and then running footsteps: *tap-tap-tap-tap-tap . . . sssssssssssssssssssssssssssssssss sssssssssssssssssssssssssssssssssssssssss . . .*

Below, a spark! It sputtered and spattered along a line.

*. . . sssssssssssssssssssssss . . .*

"DYNAMITE!" Badger yelled. He turned and raced for the rock. He scooped up Augusta as he plowed into Skunk. They landed in a heap with Badger's body over both of them.

. . . sssssssssssssssssssst.

*BA-BOOOOOOOOOM!*

# CHAPTER TWELVE

FOG. FUG. *DIRT IN SNOUT. WHERE AM I?* BADGER'S heartbeat drummed in his ears.

*Cave. Fisher. Dynamite.*

A shove against his rib cage. "Get. Off. Me. Why are badgers so heavy?"

"Bock! Bock-bock-bock." The voice (along with a beam of light) came from under his armpit.

"RRAAAAAUK!"

*DINOSAUR.* To calm himself, Badger thought: *The dinosaur is over there, on those rocks, a generous gap away.* How had he gotten into this? It was a predicament without precedent! Wasn't he supposed to be looking for a letter *A* agate for the Wall of Rocks?

Badger chuckled anxiously ("heh-heh-heh") and eased to his hind feet.

"Finally you move!" Skunk sat up. "What is so funny? It is not funny when dynamite goes off and then you are squashed by a badger." He tugged out his tricornered hat, bent it into shape, and stuck it on his head.

Augusta shook herself out and switched off her headlamp.

Badger swatted at his backside. Dust puffed; pebbles, debris, dirt rained down.

High up, Badger heard a soft crackle. He froze. His ears twitched in the direction of the sound. A pop, pop-POP. A scattershot pelting.

"ROCK!" Badger yelled, backing up. Augusta flapped onto Skunk's tricornered hat as Skunk raced after Badger.

There was a high creaking *CRACK-k-k-k*, then a sigh as the rock broke free.

Skunk and Badger flattened themselves against the wall of the cave.

A bright CLAP! as the rock struck and bounced.

"ArrrrrrRRRRAaaUCK!" cried the dinosaur.

Badger shut his eyes. *CLAP!* The rock bounced for a second horrible time. The sound ricocheted, ripped through the air, and . . .

*THUD.*

Everything chattered, including Badger's teeth.

Rocks pelted by. Dust and dirt fogged the air.

A rivulet of rubble: *Ta-da-dun, dun . . . dun . . . tunk.*

All was still.

Skunk's voice broke the silence: "What are the odds of the rock landing right there? It is like a dinosaur bridge." Badger opened his eyes and saw Skunk wearing a dusty and dirty tricornered hat. Augusta, tucked in the hat's front corner, looked more bedraggled plume than bantam hen.

Skunk pointed. Badger looked. The rock had wedged firmly in the gap between their ledge and the wall that had held the dinosaur. Skunk turned to face Badger. "I do not see a dinosaur. Do you think the dinosaur is okay?"

Close behind Skunk, a horn, then a block-like head rose as the dinosaur step-step-stepped up onto the rock-bridge. It tilted its head and looked at Badger (first with its right eye, then its left eye, then with both eyes at once).

"Fine. It's fine," Badger managed. He slid sideways along the wall of the cave. He gestured to Skunk to do the same. Skunk turned. His eyes went wide.

The dinosaur stuck its neck out to get a closer look at Skunk. "Roooooooooooop?"

The dinosaur ruffled its twig collar energetically. It hopped back and forth on its two feet. "Rawk-rawk?" It tossed its horned head in Skunk's direction. "RAWK!"

And then Badger saw it. The tricornered hat. "HORN!"

Skunk's eyes were full of terror. "I KNOW THE DINOSAUR HAS A HORN."

"NO." Badger waved his paws over his own head. "YOUR HAT. THREE HORNS. YOU LOOK LIKE A DINOSAUR!"

The dinosaur lowered its horned head.

Skunk gaped and then said, "TRI-*HORN*-ERED?"

The dinosaur galloped at Skunk.

Skunk's eyes popped wide, then slammed shut. His face screwed into a knot.

The dinosaur slid to a stop in front of Skunk. "AAAAARRRRRAAAAUUK!" it cried.

A long pink and pointy tongue licked Skunk chin to tricornered hat.

Augusta wiggled free of the hat's corner. She tilted her head (blink, left eye, right eye) and step-stepped to the hat's curled edge. She balanced there. Then she flutter-step-stepped onto the dinosaur's head. She stopped between the dinosaur's eyes. "BOCK."

"What is going on?" Badger said out loud.

The dinosaur shook its head. Augusta held on. "Bock! Bock-bock-bock."

Badger grabbed hold of Skunk and pulled him away. "I am not slurped?" Skunk mumbled, as Badger pressed his bandana into Skunk's paw and pulled off the tricornered hat. Skunk mopped himself drier, returned the damp bandana, and said with urgency, "Where is Augusta? Have you seen Augusta?"

Badger gestured toward the dinosaur.

Skunk looked. "Oh no."

Together the two of them watched Augusta lean to peer (right, left, right) into one dinosaur eye, then step-step-step across the dinosaur's snout to peer (left, up, down, left) in the other.

Skunk gave Badger an urgent look. "She has done it. She will not come down now."

"What do you mean? Done what?"

Skunk leaned forward. "Augusta has been gathering her nerve. She says no matter what happens she will go with the dinosaur. If Fisher takes the dinosaur to the zoo, the science lab, a pet store, she will go with it." Skunk shook his head. "Badger, that is a dinosaur—and not a vegetarian one either! Augusta will not be talked out of doing this. I have tried."

He looked at Augusta. His eyes grew round. "Snack-sized!"

Badger stared at Skunk in horror. "Why didn't you tell me?"

"When?" Skunk spread his paws. "Between the dynamite blast and the falling rock?"

Augusta began to sing her burbling lullaby. The dinosaur's eyes widened, and then crossed. "Roop? Roop-roop?" And then the dinosaur cooed. "Roooooooop."

Augusta's body puffed out with breath—breath spun into notes, notes built into melody. The dinosaur stared in a contented cross-eye at the tiny orange hen on its snout. "Roop-roop? Roop-roop?"

Of course, Badger understood. Hundreds of millions of years had passed. The Age of Dinosaurs? Gone with a meteoritic ka-boom! The dinosaur needed a guide, someone to show it how to follow life's trail map in the Age of Mammals. But Augusta? Badger wrung his paws. "I've only just gotten to know her. Augusta is my friend. I don't want her to do this."

Skunk sighed heavily. "I know."

Augusta fluffed, flap-flapped onto the horn on the dinosaur's head, and switched on her headlamp. "BOCK BOCK," she called out.

"GOODBYE?" Skunk exclaimed.

Badger stared at Skunk. "Goodbye? What does she mean, goodbye?"

From the top of the dinosaur a chicken-sized light beamed out. Then the dinosaur, with Augusta clinging to the horn, turned and began to stride up, up, up into the cavern.

"Where are they going?" Badger said. "The way out is down there." Badger looked where he pointed and saw only rubble, chunks of stone, and the remains of two spotlights. The passageway was completely blocked.

Augusta's burbling lullaby filled the cave as she and the dinosaur climbed higher and higher. "Roop-roop?" said the dinosaur.

"Roo-roo?" the walls of the cave echoed back.

"I am going after them," said Skunk. He pulled on his tricornered hat, his eyes trained on the beam of light. "It is not safe. There is not an exit up there. What will happen when the dinosaur gets stuck at the top with Augusta? It will not go well. I will find my courage and help out." He gave Badger a grim, determined look.

"We will go together," Badger said with a nod.

Their knapsacks were half-buried under rubble. They dug them out and strapped them on. When Badger looked up into the cavern, the light from Augusta's headlamp was now no bigger than a pinprick. Despite loose stone, the dinosaur was nimble on its feet.

"Hurry!" urged Badger.

Skunk looked up. "Yes, we must hurry!"

They followed the dinosaur and Augusta up, up, up. They used their claws. They scrambled. They clambered. They moved briskly. But still, the dinosaur was faster. It wasn't long before they lost the pinprick of light from Augusta's headlamp. After that Augusta's burbling singing could no longer be heard. Then–far, far off–they heard a *ram-ram-ramming*, a tumbling of rocks. And?

Silence.

*Augusta!* Badger picked up his pace. Skunk matched it.

Then–finally–they hugged their way around a rock face and smelled fresh air. *Fresh air?* They clambered over a boulder and saw light on a pile of rubble. They stepped into the light and looked up. Badger saw a hole filled with sky.

Badger linked his paws together and hoisted Skunk through the hole.

"SUNLIGHT!" Skunk called.

Badger secured his hind foot, placed a digging claw into a crevice, and heaved himself into . . .

*A meadow?*

He rubbed his eyes and saw a butterfly, three flowers. Bees buzzed in loops.

Badger got to his feet and scanned the area. "Where is she? Where is Augusta?"

But there was no sign of a bantam hen. Or a dinosaur.

The three flowers caught his eye. He did a double-take. *Those aren't flowers.* He picked one up and held it out to Skunk. "Look!"

Skunk examined it. "Feather—Lavender Orpington." He nodded and gestured at the meadow. "Feathers are everywhere." Skunk squatted down and pulled a lengthy cocoa-brown feather from the grasses. "Transylvania Naked Neck?"

Now Badger saw them too. Feathers tangled in the grasses; feathers caught on branches and bark; feathers rocked in the air, whittling their way to the ground. Badger pinched up a delicate black feather with a white tip.

Skunk nodded at it. "A Scots Dumpy."

Badger looked at Skunk with the question in his eyes, then he said it: "What does this mean?"

Skunk put his paws on his hips and nodded. "It is good news. The chickens came."

# CHAPTER THIRTEEN

"LUNCH!" SKUNK PLUNKED DOWN, TUGGED OFF HIS knapsack, and pulled out a lunch sack. Badger glanced at Skunk and then stared. Skunk was covered with a dusty gray particulate. Spiderwebs drifted off the tricornered hat, and the fur on his face was swirled in stiffened, mucky peaks. Badger recalled the dinosaur lick and flinched as Skunk brought a clean sandwich to his face and bit down.

After a pause, Badger said, "That's it? The chickens came so all is well? Are you sure chickens can handle a dinosaur? A dinosaur in a henhouse? How do we know Augusta is okay?"

Skunk chewed and considered. "I do not know for certain, but a meadow full of chicken feathers looks good to me, especially after what I expected." He paused, then laughed. "Ha! With all those chickens around that baby dinosaur will not get away with much! Ha-ha!"

Badger did not find this funny.

Skunk saw the look on Badger's face. "It is a mistake to underestimate chickens. Chickens continually surprise. It is the truth, Badger!" Skunk nodded and looked away. "One minute everything is dark, and you are sure the worst possible end is coming. And then—suddenly!—a spot of blue sky. How does that happen? Why does it happen? Who knows? But it does happen. It happens more often than one would expect."

Skunk sighed, and the paw that held his sandwich dropped to his lap. "It is also true that bad things—ruinous, carnivorous bad things—happen all the time. Sometimes the bad things happen to you, or your friends, or your family, and you are required to carry the weight of them. Sometimes you are certain it is The End." Skunk shook his head sadly. "Slurped up a rat."

Then he nodded. "You are right, Badger. This could end badly. Still, the chickens were here. That is a spot of blue sky. And what can we do now? Whatever took place in this meadow has already occurred."

Badger huffed.

"A note would have been nice," Skunk said. He took another bite and patted the moss next to him. "Sit. You *must* be hungry."

The sun was in its afternoon position. Badger's stomach shuddered, then shook. *Lunch!*

With much effort, Badger shoved the thought aside and scanned the area again. No chicken. No dinosaur. No sign of struggle. Feathers everywhere.

A dinosaur hatching from a fossilized egg? Impossible! As an Important Rock Scientist, he *shouldn't* believe any of it. Yet there was a hole—*right there*. Badger stared at the hole. The hole led to the cavern where he'd first seen the fossilized egg in amber.

Again Badger searched the meadow. *Where is Augusta?*

"Sludge and slurry." Badger ran a paw through his stripe and rubble showered down.

With a sigh, Badger plopped down next to Skunk and got out his lunch sack. He unwrapped his sandwich, shoved most of it into his mouth, and swallowed. Next to him, Skunk laughed. "Ha! Remember when you yelled 'Egg marks the spot?' EGG MARKS THE SPOT! Like that! Ha! Eggnotized!"

Badger sighed. "Yes, eggnotized." He did remember, but Augusta filled his thoughts. *I hope you're okay, Augusta.*

———◄o►———

After lunch, Skunk and Badger agreed that they could not stay at Campsite #5 another night. "Fisher is ruthless," said Badger.

Skunk nodded. "He will not be happy when he discovers there is no dinosaur in the cave." It was time to pack up.

They walked for an hour and a half and then arrived at the campsite. "Bath time!" Skunk called out, peeling off to follow the path to Endless Lake. Badger spotted his tent. A bath sounded nice, but they needed to leave as soon as possible. He would start by taking down the tent.

Twenty minutes later, the campsite was tidied and Badger's tent lay flattened with the stakes removed and the poles bundled. Skunk appeared at the top of the path. He'd gone from dusty gray to a wet black and white. Even the tricornered hat looked somewhat cleaner.

Skunk hop-hop-jogged over to Badger. "Everything is all taken care of!"

"Good. I'll get your backpack down." Badger headed toward the tree where the yellow SunSett Adventures backpack and the blue Heave Ho Hauler dangled in the air.

Skunk raced ahead and stepped in front of him. "Leave it. We can wait until the last minute. We do not want to invite the bears. Remember?"

Blocked, Badger stopped. Even from this distance, Skunk's yellow backpack looked all angles, corners, and sharp edges. The bellows left a distinct impression.

"Skunk, it needs to be repacked. It took you a *long time* to pack it. Remember?"

"Packing is not necessary. Everything is all taken care of," Skunk said, grinning. "I arranged for mussels."

"Muscles? Where?" Badger looked at Skunk's arms. *Puny.* He looked at Skunk's legs. *Minuscule.*

Skunk dug around in his pockets and retrieved a damp card. He held it out.

Badger read:

---

# MOVING MUSSELS
## KEEP CLAM *and*
## CARRY ON!

*The Pebbly Shoreline, Endless Lake*

---

Skunk put the card back in his pocket. "So friendly too. 'Happy to help!' was the first thing they said, and that grin—ear to ear! I did have to stick my face under the water. The water is *very* cold! Why is Endless Lake so cold in the middle of summer? Anyway, the Moving Mussels will be taking the yellow backpack to the brownstone."

"Freshwater bivalves?" It made no sense. "Two shells stuck together with a hinge?" Badger opened and shut his paws.

"Exactly! There were mussels of all sorts, but they were mostly Long Johns, Pugnose Muckets, and Pocketbooks."

Badger held up a paw. "Let me get this straight: *shells* are going to carry that yellow SunSett Adventures backpack all the way to the brownstone?"

Skunk stared at Badger and then shook his head in disbelief. "Mussels are so much more than shells! The mussels told me that some animals cannot see past the shell. Why is that? The mussel is right there! You have not met the mussels? *Ever?* But this is your favorite lake."

Badger felt a wave of weariness. It had been quite a day. He looked at Skunk. "Help me roll up my tent, okay?"

"Happy to help!" said Skunk in a funny high voice.

"Great," Badger replied flatly.

That was when he turned and saw them. There at the edge of the woods were the unmistakable tips of a pair of lemon-yellow loafers.

# CHAPTER FOURTEEN

"COUSIN!"

Skunk groaned.

Fisher stepped from shadow into light and raised his walking stick in mock salute. "I've been looking everywhere for you. But of course you're here—Campsite Number Five. Your old favorite!"

"What now, Fisher?" Badger snarled.

Fisher set his walking stick down with a thump. "Where's my dinosaur, Badger?"

Skunk's tail flicked up. "It is not *your* dinosaur. No one *owns* a dinosaur!"

Badger put a paw on Skunk's shoulder and met Fisher's amused gaze. "What's it to you?"

"Like that, is it?" Fisher gave a snort. "Let me introduce Patch and Sweet Pea."

Out of the shadow stepped two cats. One was a stringy calico with a white splotch over one eye. *Patch.* The other was a burly tiger stripe with tufts of fur missing. The tiger stripe yawned widely, got down on all fours, and stretched into a startling forward curl. With a shudder, it sheathed and unsheathed its claws. Then it got up, settled into a cool lean, and languidly licked a paw. *Not sweet. Bigger than a pea.*

"I do not like house cats out of houses," Skunk muttered. His eyes had grown big. His tail trembled.

Badger shot Fisher a steely gaze. "Your friends have gone feral, Fisher."

Sweet Pea cracked knuckles on one paw, then the other. Patch rolled a shoulder.

"Feral? I suppose. Ho-ho!" Fisher chuckled. "Sweet Pea and Patch were left loose to wander *months* ago. Maim and bat, wound and whack, mutilate, lacerate—that is a cat. And how they play! If it *rolls*, it amuses. As I always say, who am I to stop their fun?" Fisher paused, angled his head, and said, "I repeat: Where is my dinosaur?"

The cats lowered onto all fours, their tails slicing the air.

Badger frowned. "How do I know? Your guess is as good as mine."

Fisher clicked his tongue. "That isn't good enough."

Badger's heart thumped. "Where do you think I'm hiding a dinosaur?" He gestured at Campsite #5. "What you see is what you get."

"You're not telling me everything. Let me persuade you to be more forthcoming." Fisher flicked his chin. Patch and Sweet Pea crept forward. Patch went one way. Sweet Pea went the other.

Skunk stepped back. Badger stepped back with him and held up his paws. "Come on, Fisher. You don't have a dinosaur. I don't have an amber egg for science. We've both been unlucky. Let's call this off, all right?"

To Badger's left, Skunk shifted restlessly and breathed in bursts, but Badger could not risk a glance. The cats were closing in. Patch stalked Skunk. Sweet Pea crept closer, then closer.

Fisher rapped his walking stick against the ground, then looked up with a grin. "I don't want to ruffle any feathers, but where is that little orange ball of fluff?"

Skunk went rigid. "We will not talk about her!" And then, in a sudden burst of speed, Skunk took off like a shot. The tricornered hat flew off his head.

*Let me introduce Patch and Sweet Pea.*

"CATS!" Badger yelled in alarm. "CHASE REFLEX!" Cat brains allow cats one option in cases like this: chase!

In a single leap, Sweet Pea covered half the distance. Patch raced in the other direction. Badger ran after them. Fisher followed.

Skunk stopped near the tall tree. He pulled something out of his pocket and threw it to Badger.

Badger caught it.

Skunk made a chopping gesture and looked UP.

Badger looked at what he held. *A spatula?* He eyed the rope that held the backpacks in the air. *With a spatula?* But what choice did he have? As if he held an axe, Badger gritted his teeth and ("AAAaaaUUGH!") swung the edge of the spatula at the rope.

It should never have worked.

But it did!

The rope was severed, cut in two. (*By a spatula? Yes, a spatula!*) The spatula embedded itself in the tree trunk. Badger let go and stepped away. (There was no time to marvel.) The rope whirred into the tree with a *zzzzhhhhhhhhh!*

At the sound, Patch let out a whine. Sweet Pea swatted at the air. Fisher hunched in a cower.

The backpacks fell.

Badger's Heave Ho Hauler *THUNK*ed next to Fisher, who jumped and slipped. The SunSett Adventures backpack caught on a branch, tipped over, and—*broken strap!*—the lid flipped open. First came the cast-iron frying pan, then the bag of chicken feed, pretzels, and a dozen pre-packed lunch sacks. A garlic press hammered. Eggs burst. A soy sauce bottle smashed. The beak of the bellows speared the ground, planting the bellows upright. And then the yellow SunSett Adventures backpack flipped free and landed with a soft *thwomp*.

There was a pause, followed by the sound of clapping. Badger looked.

Fisher clapped his paws, an amused smile dancing on his furry face. *Clap-clap.* "Nice try! Quite a little plan!" *Clap-clap.* "Was that a spatula? Ho-ho! Who knew?" *Clap. Clap. Clap.*

Badger took stock of the situation and backed up. Patch and Sweet Pea were close—too close! Skunk was much farther off— over there. Badger took another step backward.

Fisher's gaze pierced. "Time's up. Tell me what happened in the cave." He jerked his head, and Patch and Sweet Pea moved in.

Skunk moved with them. "Do not touch Badger!"

"Skunk, get out of here! Back off slowly!" Badger hissed.

A slight sound above him. A crumple of paper. And then: *poof . . . Poof . . . POOF . . .*

*POOOOOOOOOOOOOFFFFFFFFFFFFFF!*

The five-pound bag of flour exploded. The air was fogged with finely milled wheat. Skunk disappeared from sight. Badger dove for the ground. Patch leapt after Badger. Badger flipped around and snapped his teeth.

With a punch, Skunk broke through the floury fog. He landed between Patch and Badger, lifted his tail, and sprayed Patch with precision.

"MAAAAHRRrrr!" Patch yowled and leapt off.

"In the kisser!" Skunk said, raising a clenched paw.

The stink! *That* stink! Badger nearly gagged, and yet it was the stink of hope. His eyes watered. His snout dripped. But none of this mattered. He jumped to his feet, covered his face, and gestured wildly at Skunk. "Spray Sweet Pea! SPRAY THEM ALL."

Skunk stumbled over and latched on to Badger's elbow. "Have I mentioned spraying makes me sleepy? I need a nap." He sagged onto the ground.

"A nap? NOW?"

But Skunk was asleep where he lay.

A distant jingling. Badger barely paid it any attention. He positioned himself in front of Skunk and thought, *I will stay and defend Skunk—whatever comes.*

What came was Sweet Pea—with paws swinging. A left cuff! Badger hooked the cat with a claw. The jingling grew louder. Sweet Pea buffeted Badger's hind foot. Badger swung his digging claws and smelled something minty. *Mint? In all this skunk spray?* Still—*yes!*—the air smelled somewhat fresher.

A shudder ran through Sweet Pea. The cat scratched wildly, then batted at a dust mote above its head. The smell of mint grew stronger, along with the sound of jingling.

"Concentrate!" Fisher commanded the cat.

Panting, Sweet Pea cast a pained look at Fisher, and then the cat flipped onto its back and twitched frantically.

"Are those sleigh bells?" Skunk mumbled behind Badger.

Badger looked. The forest floor seemed to be moving. No, wait! It was lots of somethings—no, some*ones*—moving across the forest floor. Was that greenery tied to tails? Then Badger understood.

"SCRATCH," Badger yelled. Scratch led a charge of rats—hundreds and hundreds of rats—across Campsite #5. They'd tied bells and greenery to their tails. Some of the rats wore ball caps emblazoned with the number 73.

Scratch raised her paw in greeting. "CATNIP. GOOD LUCK."

"I OWE YOU ONE," Badger yelled.

Scratch jabbed her tail at Fisher. "EXPECT A LETTER FROM ROSHA." Then Scratch disappeared from sight into Rat Guild 73.

Sweet Pea bucked onto all fours and ("MEAAAHRrr!") galloped after them.

The cats were gone.

Badger heaved a sigh of relief. It was done. He looked at his cousin. "I don't have your dinosaur. Go home, Fisher."

With that, Badger turned to Skunk. Skunk slept where he had crumpled, his mouth half open. Badger tugged Skunk into a more comfortable position.

But Fisher did not leave. Fisher stayed put. He stood behind Badger and began to speak: "What does she see in you? Why did you get the brownstone? You're crusty, cantankerous. Where's the charm? Where's the panache? Do you know how many rocks *I've* found? Rocks with real value. Rocks that bring animals to blows! You should have seen the vein of opals I discovered last spring. And that's not the half of it! I can find anything. Finding a dinosaur is nothing! I'm top of the treasure trade. Everyone knows Fisher. Who knows you, Badger? Rock science! The chipping away at the most ordinary of rocks—day in, day out. Why does Aunt Lula care?"

Badger heard the sound first. *Smack*. It was the sound of a rock being tossed and caught. Toss, *smack*. Toss, *smack*. A memory surfaced—the Weasel Family Reunion. With his back to Fisher, Badger said, "I didn't *get* the brownstone. Aunt Lula is *letting* me and Skunk live there." In front of him, Skunk yawned and curled into a ball.

*Smack*, Badger heard.

Badger got to his feet and turned around.

The Spider Eye Agate lay in Fisher's paw. Whirls and eyes! Dark hidden depths! Badger stared and then looked at Fisher with genuine confusion. "You've had it all this time? Why? You don't like agates."

Fisher shrugged. "Why not? I've got it. You don't." He shot Badger a look. "Want it?"

Badger *wanted* it. To feel the agate in his paws one more time? To gaze into it and imagine the birth of Planet Earth? His Spider Eye Agate was the rock that had begun it all! "That is *my* rock. I found it. Give it back!" Badger reached for the agate.

Fisher closed his claws around it and put his paw behind his back. "Tell me what happened after the dynamite went off. Where's the hen? Tell me or you'll never see your agate again."

Badger knew there should not be a choice to make. Betray Augusta—*and* the other chickens, and the dinosaur—for an agate? He knew this should not be something he had to think about! But Badger wanted his agate back. He'd wanted his agate for a very long time. It was—and always would be—his letter *A* rock.

"AannnNNH!" Badger moaned through clenched teeth.

It was at this moment that Badger heard something behind him: "Humpf. Hm." *Plod, plod.* "Huh."

*Skunk!* Skunk sounded groggy, but he was right there, behind Badger. *I am not alone. I am with my friend.*

*Plod.* The ground shuddered. "Hummpff."

*Yes! Together we stand!* Behind him, Badger felt puffs of stale breath parting his fur, along with a radiating heat. *The heat of my friend standing close!* Badger straightened his shoulders. He adjusted his footing. He pushed out his chest. "You can't defeat the two of us, Fisher!" And then Badger finally said what needed to be said: "Keep the agate. I'm keeping my friends."

The response was quick. (And so satisfying!) A look of fright appeared on Fisher's face. He gave a yip, fell to the ground, then scrambled backwards. In the process, the Spider Eye Agate dropped from his paw. Fisher got to his feet, pointed at Badger, and said, "This isn't over. You and your friends haven't heard the last of me."

With a backward glance, Fisher dashed into the woods.

The bear hurtled over Badger and landed (*thud*).

"BEAR?" said Badger. Bears also had a chase reflex! Badger yelled out, "DON'T RUN." (Fisher was his cousin, after all.) But it was too late: Fisher was fleeing at full speed.

The bear pursued Fisher for two or three leaps, then slid to a stop. "Huh! Huh!" the bear huffed.

Fisher ran on.

The bear's enormous head swung around and surveyed all that lay under the tree. The bear returned at a trot. *Plod-d-plod-d-plod.*

Badger scrambled backwards and tripped on Skunk.

Skunk rubbed his eyes. "Did I miss anything?"

Badger pointed.

*Thump.* The bear sat.

"OH," said Skunk.

Skunk and Badger watched the bear lift the yellow SunSett Adventures backpack high into the air and shake it. Several granola bar chunks, a cherry pitter, and a panini press fell out.

The bear tossed the backpack aside and put its snout in a lunch sack. "Hmm. Hummus."

"VERY big. BEARS. Big," said Skunk with a squeak.

Badger could only nod.

———◄◦►———

They left the bear under the tall tree, sitting on the exploded flour wrapper and gulping down sandwiches from the pre-packed lunch sacks. A bottle of Sriracha sauce, a bag of raisins, three onions, and a smashed Blue Hubbard squash rested near the bear's hind feet. "It is a bear buffet," Skunk declared.

Badger found his Spider Eye Agate. He picked it up and held it in his cupped paws. He lifted it into the last rays of sunlight and ("Har-har!") imagined the birth of Planet Earth. He showed Skunk. "That is something to see!" said Skunk. Yes, holding his Spider Eye Agate brought back memories. And then Badger carried his agate down to the shores of Endless Lake.

"Are you sure you want to do this, Badger?" Skunk said. "This is the best agate you have *ever* found. It is your letter *A* agate for the Wall of Rocks. It would be sad if you had regrets."

Badger rolled his Spider Eye Agate in his paws and sighed. The waves of Endless Lake *washhhhh-washhhhh*ed against the

shore. "Ow! ah-Wow," called a ring-billed gull. "Ow! ah-Wow.
Ow, ow, ow."

Badger looked at his agate and said, "But if I don't do this,
I'll worry that Fisher will take it again. I'll spend my life trying
to keep it from Fisher. I have Important Rock Work to do. How
will I find my focus, focus, focus? And what if Fisher takes it
again? Perhaps next time I'll choose the agate instead of my
friends. This agate has done me a lot of good. Where would I
be without it? But now it needs to go back where it came from."

Skunk thought a moment, and then laughed. "Ha! Perhaps another young badger will find it and also become an Important Rock Scientist."

"Yes! Har-har!" And so, with all his strength, Badger threw the Spider Eye Agate back into Endless Lake.

The agate went up.

The agate went down.

*Ka-SPLOOSH!*

# CHAPTER FIFTEEN

ON THURSDAY, SKUNK AND BADGER WOKE UP IN THEIR own beds in Aunt Lula's brownstone. It was late. By the time they had finished their breakfasts, it was three o'clock in the afternoon. So it was four o'clock when they opened the front door and found the yellow SunSett Adventures backpack leaning against the brownstone. It had been neatly packed.

There was a business card. Badger picked it up and read:

## MOVING MUSSELS
### Never underestimate
### your local bivalve!

*The Pebbly Shoreline, Endless Lake*

*Two shells with a hinge? How?* Wisely, Badger did not say this out loud.

Inside the pack, Skunk found nearly everything he had left behind at Campsite #5. In fact, Skunk did not seem to be missing anything except what had been eaten. "My tricornered hat, and . . . the spatula! How did they get the spatula out of the tree trunk?" He flexed it. "Thin and flippy. A spatula for the ages!" He pocketed it with a grin. "Moving Mussels are the best!"

"Ahem." Badger cleared his throat. "Do you think you'll be using the yellow SunSett Adventures backpack?"

"NO," Skunk said emphatically. "ABSOLUTELY NOT. A pack for your back? HA! I will not be falling for *that* again."

"I'd be happy to take it off your paws," Badger said quickly.

Skunk looked at him like he was crazy, then considered. "You can have it!"

So Badger took it. "Thank you. Thank you very much!"

*A backpack made by badgers for badgers*, thought Badger as he brought it up to his rock room.

———◦———

On Friday, Skunk twisted his paws. He jumped at small sounds. Sunday was only two days away. "It will be a Sunday without the *New Yak Times Book Review*. It is a big loss, but what can I do? Mr. G. Hedgehog!" He nodded to himself and padded down the hallway.

This gave Badger an idea.

———◀◦▶———

The next day, Saturday, Badger walked to Chicken Books and placed a subscription to the Sunday *New Yak Times*. He put it in his own name. "Badger," he said loudly with much enunciation. He had no "previous arrangement" with Mr. G. Hedgehog, so the hedgehog would not take the *Book Review*. Badger gave his address: "Ms. Lula P. Marten's brownstone in North Twist." *It will be a surprise*, he thought with a smile.

———◀◦▶———

The next morning, Skunk plunked a bowl of half-cooked oatmeal in front of Badger, then groaned and slumped in his seat. He strained to lift his head to look at Badger. "I am not hungry. I do not want to read, or play card games, or go to Chicken Books, or meet new animals at the farmers' market. Shopping! How could I look at fruit and vegetables at a time like this? In fact, there is so much I do not want to do that there is nothing to do." He looked at Badger with wide eyes. "Nothing to do!"

Skunk set his head on the table.

It took Badger a moment to realize it was Sunday. The Sunday *New Yak Times*!

Badger rushed to the front door and opened it. "Ah-ha!" There it was! On the front stoop lay a newspaper wrapped in brown paper. Badger seized it and raced back. He dropped it— *thunk*—on the kitchen table.

Skunk lifted his head. "What? How? Badger!" Skunk grinned. He tore off the paper wrapper and the newspaper fell open. He spread the newspaper across the kitchen table and dug through it. Skunk mumbled as he tossed whole sections aside: "Arts and Leisure . . . Style . . . Sunday Review . . . Sports . . . the Magazine." Then he frowned. "Where is it?" He went pale under his fur. A slight nod. "I will do it again, but slower."

Badger held his breath and watched Skunk open each section and examine it page by page, by page . . . to the last page.

Skunk's eyes darted. He muttered, "This is what happens. It happens *every* time. Mr. G. Hedgehog! The *New Yak Times Book Review* is GONE."

Skunk's head fell into his paws.

"It is *my* subscription!" Badger growled. "This will not do!"

137

Skunk's voice rose in a monotone from the table: "The *Book Review* will be found—*eventually*. Under the rhododendron. In the recycle bin. Have I mentioned the toeless boot?"

He had!

Badger stormed to the front door, tossed it open, and—

*And what exactly?*

Everything looked as it always did. Morning dewdrops glinted in the meadow across the way. "Wheep-wheep-wheep-wheep-wheep!" called a cardinal. Nothing was amiss, except for what was missing.

Then Badger heard: *Crinkle. Snap-snap! Crinkle-crinkle.*

Badger tip-clawed, tip-clawed to the edge of the stoop, leaned over, and saw the hedge. Through the hedge he glimpsed red plaid and a tassel.

Badger returned to the kitchen with a small hedgehog wearing a red plaid tam o'shanter cap. The hedgehog also wore a shamefaced blush. Badger gave the hedgehog a pat at the doorway and announced, "The *New Yak Times Book Review* is found."

With his head down, Mr. G. Hedgehog pad-pad-padded his way across the kitchen, climbed onto a chair, and set the *Book Review* on the kitchen table. He looked at Skunk. "I apologize. I thought we had an agreement."

Skunk huffed. "Agreement? When did we agree? I do not remember saying you could take my *Book Review*."

"Oh dear." The hedgehog squirmed one way, then the other.

"Hm! Yes, there is that." Badger winced as he watched.

Skunk leaned forward. "Why would you do it? Why would you take my *Book Review* without asking?"

Mr. G. Hedgehog tugged fitfully at his tam o'shanter and met Skunk's gaze. "At first, I told myself I was only borrowing the *Book Review*. I saw the Sunday *New Yak Times* lying in its wrapper on the pavement. I told myself I would take a peek at the *Book Review* and put it right back. Putting it back proved difficult."

Skunk nodded with urgency. "Pawprints on the wrapper!"

Mr. G. Hedgehog examined his paws, and quickly stuffed them into his pockets. His pace picked up as he continued: "After that I told myself you knew but didn't care. I clambered up and retrieved it from the 'Peaches in Syrup' can—"

"And left it under the rhododendron!" Skunk interjected.

Mr. G. Hedgehog flushed under his fur and words spilled out: "Finally, I said to myself, 'Skunk has never said anything about it. This is an unspoken agreement.' Around that time there were so many water sprinklers going off unexpectedly that I took to carrying the *Book Review* in a—"

"Toeless boot!" Skunk said.

"Yes," said Mr. G. Hedgehog with a final nod.

Skunk sighed heavily. He looked at Mr. G. Hedgehog (who was now slouched in his seat) and said: "I should have said something. We could have gotten to the bottom of this situation sooner." Skunk tilted his head at Badger. "You were right. I had not tried everything."

"Ah," said Badger, who did not know what else to say.

Mr. G. Hedgehog sat up. His gaze settled on Skunk. "It wasn't mine to take! I apologize, Skunk. I will not take your *Book Review* again." The hedgehog nodded to himself. "The *New Yak Times Book Review* is a weakness. I devour book reviews with the same relish as the books themselves. This stops NOW."

Skunk stared. "You do? You like book reviews that much? Really?"

Mr. G. Hedgehog blinked up at him as if surprised to find Skunk there. "Yes. It doesn't excuse my behavior, however. This will not happen again."

Skunk leaned forward. "It is the thrill of the hunt. Sometimes you find the perfect book for Long Story Night."

The hedgehog's eyes widened. He nodded vigorously. "Sometimes it is enough to *imagine* all the enjoyment you would get from reading this or that book."

Skunk slapped the kitchen table. "Yes!"

"And yaks!" Mr. G. Hedgehog said excitedly. "Yaks know how to review books. Yaks are passionate about books and reading. Yaks write with style, originality, and humor." He held up a claw. "Also, yaks reveal their likes and dislikes so you know *why* they hold an opinion, which allows you to disagree with them more easily." Mr. G. Hedgehog raised an eyebrow. "Yaks are respectful of their readers."

Skunk's jaw hung open for a moment, and then: "Ha! I thought it was the shaggy bangs and the hump of nutrients—you know, for focus and not having to eat all that often."

Mr. G. Hedgehog shrugged conspiratorially. "Can't hurt."

"You like the *Book Review* as much as I do!" exclaimed Skunk.

There was a pause as Skunk and the hedgehog grinned at each other.

Mr. G. Hedgehog patted the table. "Well, enjoy it." He climbed off the chair and started to go and then stopped. He dug around in a pocket and pulled out a folded square of newsprint. "Page twelve. Bottom left." He set it on the seat of the chair and looked up at Skunk. "Again—my apologies."

Mr. G. Hedgehog glanced at Badger and left the kitchen.

"Mr. G. Hedgehog!" Skunk called. "Would you like a pear and ginger nib muffin? I am about to make them."

And this was the beginning. From then on, Mr. G. Hedgehog came over every Sunday for Sunday breakfast and the *Book Review*. There were rules: The *Book Review* remained on the kitchen table. No ripping. Passionate discussion about books was strongly encouraged.

———◦———

Mr. G. Hedgehog wasn't the only arrival that Sunday. In the afternoon, Badger heard Skunk in the backyard, saying "I do not think so. Badger will not like it. It was difficult enough when I moved in." He went to investigate. Skunk was speaking to Scratch.

"Badger will not like what?" Badger called out as he approached.

Skunk turned around with a pained look on his face.

Scratch stepped forward with her paw on the head of a tiny rat.

"This is Zeno," said Scratch. Zeno jumped forward and tapped Badger on the shin.

Badger looked down.

"You have a rock tumbler." The tiny rat looked up with expectation.

Another voice: "You have a rock tumbler?" A second tiny rat jumped out. The rat's eyes were wide with wonder. "Can I see that?"

Scratch looked at the second tiny rat. "It's 'may I,' not 'can I.'" Scratch grinned at Badger. "This is Zephyr. You gotta teach 'em while you're able. Zeno and Zephyr were, ah, recently orphaned."

Badger sighed and then met Scratch's gaze. "I owe you one," he said, repeating the words he had called out at Campsite #5. "Thank you for coming to my rescue back there." He rested a paw on Zephyr's tiny head. "I meant what I said. But when they're grown, they move out of the brownstone. And I mean *out*—not into the walls or under the floorboards." Badger looked between Scratch and Skunk.

"Deal." Scratch flashed him her yellow-toothed grin and put out her paw.

Badger shook it.

Zeno and Zephyr blinked up at them.

Scratch glanced at her shadow. "How time flies! I gotta scrabble." Then Scratch knelt down in front of Zeno and Zephyr and gave them each a hug. "I'll be around if you need me. Remember Rat Guild 73 always has room for two quality rats like you."

The two tiny rats nodded seriously.

And then Scratch and Skunk said goodbye and pounded each other on the back.

Zeno, Zephyr, Skunk, and Badger watched Scratch leave. Halfway across the backyard, Scratch turned. "Barbecue soon, all right, kid? Let's get that number-ten tin-can stove smoking!"

"Ha! Yes!" Skunk waved.

Scratch unlatched the back gate and disappeared down the alley.

Badger felt someone tap his shin again. He looked down. "Where's the rock tumbler?" said Zephyr. Zeno's eyes widened.

"Ah, why don't you move in first?" said Badger.

(That evening, Badger made a do-not-enter sign for his rock room door.)

———◄◦►———

On Monday, Skunk gave Badger a chunk of amber. "It occurred to me that amber starts with the letter *A*." Skunk rotated the amber chunk and tapped his claw on a spot. "There is a chip of dinosaur shell in it. See?"

Badger took it from Skunk. "Egg marks the spot," he said quietly.

"Do you like it? You have been playing many minor chords on your ukulele. I did not know a ukulele could sound so sad."

"I have?" Badger said. He had been playing his ukulele when he was supposed to be working on his Great Unconformity article for *Rock Hound Weekly*. He'd titled his article "Lost a Billion Years Recently? I Know Where to Find Them," but whenever he tried to write the rest, the words wouldn't come. So instead, Badger had picked up his ukulele and plucked out the kind of melodies that came to mind when one thought of a small, snack-sized chicken who goes off with a dinosaur.

Badger considered the chunk of amber in his paw and his eyes welled up. "It's perfect. Every time I look at it, I will think of her and how . . ." Badger mopped his eyes and continued: "How brave and good and courageous she was." He stopped and looked at Skunk with wide eyes. "Do you think she's okay?"

Skunk's face fell. "I have not heard a word. I think so. I hope so. I have seen chickens (a leghorn, an Australorp with an Appenzeller, three Bassettes, and Larry the Rooster), but none of them would say anything. It is worrying."

"A dinosaur?" Badger shook his head. "In a henhouse?"

"I know," said Skunk.

Badger looked at the empty stand at the beginning of the
Wall of Rocks. He took the stand down, set the chunk of amber
on it, and put it on his rock table. He glanced at Skunk. "I want
to look at it while I do Important Rock Work–until I know she
is okay."

# THE DAYS PASSED

THE DAYS BECAME WEEKS.

Then one evening (after Zeno and Zephyr had gone to their bunk beds) Badger heard a knock on his bedroom door. He opened his door and found Skunk.

Skunk held a shoebox. "This was on the front stoop."

"A chicken's shoebox?"

Skunk nodded. "I have not opened it yet."

"Is it?" Badger looked at Skunk.

"I hope so," said Skunk. He held the shoebox out. "Take off the lid."

Badger quickly removed the lid. Inside the box he saw two feathers—a tiny orange feather next to a long, twiggy one.

Badger stared. He wanted to believe it was good news, but

feathers left behind? Feathers left behind could mean a lot of things. Then he noticed some lines—some scratches, really—on the lid. Badger pointed. "Does this mean something?"

Skunk peered. "Chicken scratch." He nodded at Badger. "It takes a certain kind of squint."

Skunk took the lid from him, winched his face into a twist, and stared. After a long, tense moment, his face fell. "AaUK! I cannot do it. It still looks like a pile of sticks!"

"Let me try," said Badger, taking hold of the lid. He fixed his gaze on the marks. He squinted hard. He tilted his head and looked at it sideways.

Nothing.

Badger was about to give up, when an idea came. *Why not?* With a nod, Badger looked with his left eye. Then his right eye. Now his left. He blink-blinked. When he opened his eyes, the lines had sorted. "Har-har!"

"What?" said Skunk, pulling on his elbow.

"All is well. It says, 'ALL IS WELL!'"

"YES!" whooped Skunk.

And they both leapt for joy.

# ACKNOWLEDGMENTS

A FEW SOURCES NEED TO BE MENTIONED: HUEVOS Motuleños is a dish I eat with regularity at Frontera Grill in Chicago. It is, as Skunk declares, "one of the best breakfasts ever invented," and is the only breakfast that regularly turns up in my dreams. Badger's song "Eons" would not have been written without Stephen Marshak's textbook *Essentials of Geology: Fifth Edition*. Badger's expedition gear rules are Colin Fletcher's rules from *The Complete Walker IV* (Alfred A. Knopf, 2002). And finally, I have relied on Chris Pellant's *Rocks and Minerals* (Dorling Kindersley, 2002) to write these stories. Interested in Important Rock Work? Start here.

And now, the people: Thanks to everyone at Algonquin Young Readers and Workman Publishing. What a team! It is 2020 as I write this. Remember the 2020 pandemic? Despite all the pandemic threw in front of these folks, every one of them worked diligently and with unflagging good humor and resourcefulness. It was impressive. Thank you! Also, Elise Howard, Jon Klassen, and Steven Malk? Like the Moving Mussels, I don't quite understand how you do what you do, but you are the best! As for you, Phil: Thanks for making this project (and the rest of my life) so much fun!